the MAN SHOW

ON TAP

A Guide to All Things Beer

By Ray James

Illustrated by Rick Tulka

SIMON SPOTLIGHT ENTERTAINMENT
New York London Toronto Sydney

This is a humor book based on a T.V. show. Readers are strongly discouraged from trying this stuff at home, or even away from home. Be smart, be safe, drink carefully.

SIMON SPOTLIGHT ENTERTAINMENT
An imprint of Simon & Schuster
1230 Avenue of the Americas, New York, New York 10020

First Edition 10 9 8 7 6 5 4 3 2 1

Library of Congress Cataloging-in-Publication Data
James, Ray, 1964-
The man show on tap: a guide to all things beer / by Ray James.--1st ed. p. cm.
ISBN 0-689-87371-9
1. Beer--Humor. I. Title. PN6231.B43J36 2004   818'.607--dc22   2004005870

Table of Contents

INTRODUCTION

If you've picked up this book,

chances are you have more than a passing interest in beer, or breasts. Luckily this book is for guys who like both, perhaps more than they should.

The Man Show on Tap: A Guide to All Things Beer is meant to be a layman's guide to all beers great and small, honoring their creation, history, and the special place they hold in the hearts of Men.

Okay, confession time. No book can cover *all* things beer. The topic is much too vast. Reading a book that covered all things beer would leave no time for *drinking* beer. That title was just to get our foot in your consumer door.

There are plenty of other books out there that can tell you anything you need to know about fermentation or what temperature is best for storing an eisbock brew. *The Man Show on Tap* promises not to hurt your brain with too much of that stuff. Still, if you don't know a lager from a krausenbier, this book can help you . . . a little. But if you're looking for advice on proper keg party etiquette, or how to twist off a bottle cap with your eye socket, it should be just the ticket.

If everything goes according to plan, this book will make you appreciate beer in ways you haven't before. After all, the craft of brewing is a development that separates Man from lower primates. Okay, maybe the ability to make beer is no more "human" than developing domesticated crops, a systemized code of law, a theory of an afterlife, or unexpected plot twists in reality TV storylines. But the point is, *we* have beer and the monkeys don't. And if the sheer explosion of beer-related deaths in cases of monkey-on-man violence has taught us anything, it's to *keep* it that way.

Oh, and by the way. This is a funny book, and just like on TV, there is a lot of stuff in here you should NOT try at home. If you're stupid enough to actually put a bottle in your butt or your eye, put down this book and get some life insurance—your days are numbered. Friends don't let friends drive drunk, they don't drive friends while drunk, but, if sober, occasionally drive drunk friends. Drink responsibly, if for no other reason, the chance to drink again.

BEER THROUGH THE AGES

Depending on whom you believe, beer brewing was practiced in Egypt and Mesopotamia somewhere between five thousand and fifteen thousand years ago. The Egyptians invented many beer styles, including one known in the Nubian tongue as *boosa,* from which we get our modern word *booze.* Egyptian records show that the licensing and regulation of beer shops began as early as 1300 BC—which means the first police bribe occurred about twenty minutes later.

The Egyptians passed their knowledge on to the Greeks. Or, if you've taken first-semester African-American Studies, the Greeks *stole* it. The Greeks, in turn, taught their Italian friends to make beer, which the Romans called *cerevisia.* Their word came from Ceres, the goddess of agriculture, and *vis,* Latin for "strength." Anyone who's been in Mexico long enough to get his wallet stolen will recognize this word's Spanish cousin, *cerveza,* which loosely comes from *cer,* to "serve," and *veza,* meaning "with lime and a burrito."

Though it's seen earliest in the Fertile Crescent, brewing happened independently all over the world. When the Roman legions began draining their bladders on the British Isles (55 BC), the Britons were already getting solidly pissed on an ale they made from barley. When Columbus arrived in the New World, the Indians were making beer from corn and black birch sap. Whether you view the arrival of Europeans in the Americas as a good or a bad thing, one thing is certain: Indians can't drink.

Surprisingly, in almost all of these early cultures, brewing was women's work, most likely because vacuums and toilet brushes hadn't been invented yet. Even today, in tribal communities across the globe, women still make beer. Amazonian folklore has it that a woman was tricked into making the first beer. Even Saint Brigid was alleged to have changed bathwater into beer for a colony of thirsty lepers.

You can believe myths if you so choose, but if the chick is hot enough, lepers and non-lepers alike will gladly *guzzle* her bathwater. This is probably something guys did before they figured out how to sniff panties.

Once brewing became a commercial enterprise, however, it became mostly a male domain. Freed from the drudgery of brewing, women now had more time to raise children, cook meals, and complain to their friends about their husband's inability to communicate.

According to cultural anthropologist and beer historian Alan Eames, the Vikings were "the most beer-drunken people that ever lived." In Viking legend, Valhalla is essentially a giant alehouse where the dead feasted, and where they could drink ale as it forever streamed from the udder of a mythic goat named Heidrun. At least they were *told* it was ale . . . and an udder. To the Vikings and Anglo-Saxons, ale was more than the diamond lane to blessed intoxication. Because they lacked refrigeration and anything close to a 1.6 gpf toilet, their heat-brewed beverages were also a carb-loaded source of nourishment and a dookie-free substitute for the drinking water of the day. Teutonic brides drank beer after their wedding ceremony as an aphrodisiac. Such is the power of beer. Even in the days when one could have simply clubbed a woman on the head and had his way, the preferred method for lovers has always been to get her drunk.

During the reign of England's Henry VIII, ladies at court were allowed a daily ration of a gallon of ale. And it's widely known that Henry enjoyed a six-pack of wives. It's also been said Queen Elizabeth I liked bread and ale for breakfast and would often put away a brew "so strong as there is no man able to drink it," which is why she never got laid.

In the colonies, beer actually changed the course of history. Here's something you didn't learn in school: The reason the *Mayflower* landed at Plymouth on or about December 16, 1620, is because they'd run out of beer. And I quote from the ship's log: *"We could not now take time for further searche or consideration: our victuals being much spente, especially our beere . . ."* Yeah, once you run out of beer, you can see how spending eight weeks knocking around on the high seas in a ship overcrowded with sickly, puking prudes who desperately need a bath might lose some of its magic. Not to mention Miles Standish telling you to "knock off the coveting" every time you try to sneak a peek at Constance Hopkins while she takes a dump off the stern.

During the Industrial Revolution, German immigrants (Anheuser-Busch, Miller, Coors, Stroh, Schlitz, and Pabst) introduced lager to the States. In the 1890s, as large, regional breweries began to emerge, Pabst became the first brewer to sell over one million barrels in a year—most of it to one Midwestern fraternity.

Between 1920 and 1933, Prohibition drove all but the biggest and most adaptable brewers out of business. Anheuser-Busch switched to producing truck bodies, barley malt syrup, and ice cream. There was even a de-alcoholized version of Budweiser, known today as Budweiser.

In 1935, once the long national nightmare of Prohibition was behind us, the United States made perhaps its single greatest contribution to the history of brewing—the beer can. It was created by the American Can Company and Krueger Brewing. Though nobody remembers Krueger beer, Gottfried Krueger went on to make a killing in can openers . . . or at least he should have.

Since the mid-1980s our country has experienced a renaissance of the independent brewer. For the discerning beer fan, microbreweries are filling a niche that went unattended for decades by the megabrewers. Now, much like in the nineteenth century heyday of American brewing, you can travel to any state in the union, find a small brewpub, and pay six bucks for a beer that tastes like a pine-scented car deodorizer. It's great to be back.

THE TAO OF BEER

A great man once said

the world can be divided into two groups: beer drinkers and everybody else. He said it when he was writing the *The Man Show on Tap: A Guide to All Things Beer* and needed something bold for his *introduction*. He later thought it over and realized it was kind of cliché and stupid, so he decided to bury that observation in the body of the book near a picture of a girl with huge tits.

Which brings us to the beer lover's lifestyle. Beer drinkers the world over share a common love for their personal brew that affects the way they drink, think, dress, and talk. The next several pages will help you choose the path of how to live your life around beer. After that, you're on your own.

BOTTLE V. CAN

In life, beer drinkers may face many choices, but one of the first forks you'll come to in the road is whether to drink your brew from a bottle or a can. Maybe the choice has already been made for you, because your brand comes in a can, but not in a bottle. But let's say, as a hypothetical, you walk into the store and they have your brand in both bottles *and* cans. You're going to have to choose one or the other, and which one you go with could say a lot about you. Here are some criteria that may help you decide which camp you fall in.

Weight

The typical bottle and can of beer carry about 12 ounces, so they're even there. But bottles are heavier than cans. They take up more room. You can't fit as many in the cooler, or in the trunk of your Civic for that matter. On the other hand, the increased heft of a glass bottle just may give you a little more "Sez me!" in a bar fight. But then again if, like John Belushi's Bluto in *Animal House,* you're prone to smashing your beer container against your head, you may want to go with the can.

Round goes to: *Too close to call.*

Beer Delivery Rate

Unless you're one of those freaky beer "deep throaters" who can pour beer directly into your stomach, the BDR round goes to the can. You can shotgun a can of beer. It forces you to drink faster. With bottles, beer creates a vacuum at the top when you invert them, slowing your guzzle speed. There is no vacuum when you pop the top on that shotgun, just Newton's law of gravity doing its thing to get you wasted. Want to guzzle even *faster* from the can? Make a bigger hole in the side.

But bottle enthusiasts have turned to high technology to address this problem and created the Big Bertha of beer delivery, the 40-ounce, which has a wide enough spout to off-set the bottle's "vacuum drag coefficient" and even take on the latest in can technology—the massive shotgunned 24-ounce can.

Round goes to: *Tie.*

Empties

A throne that faces the TV and is made entirely of Lone Star bottles would be a danger-ous piece of furniture for even the most nimble pledge. However, with a little creativity and a hot glue gun, such a thing made of Olympia cans would be a handy and attractive addition to any fraternity.

But if you're planning on filling your empties with gasoline and rags to burn down the ROTC building, the bottle is your only real choice here.

Round goes to: *Even.*

Taste

Some say canned beer takes on the flavor of the can, whereas bottled beer remains untainted. Seems plausible, yet that same guy goes to the ballpark and drinks bottled beer out of a wax cup.

Round goes to: *Bottle may win on taste, but gets disqualified for wax cup. No decided advantage.*

Cost

Here canned beer seems to have a slight edge. Some of the premium, and thus more expen-sive, beers aren't even available in cans, which should give cans greater popularity. But thanks to the combined efforts Dixie beer's long-neck bottle and the great and drunken state of Louisiana, bottled beer consumption balances out all the canned beer sucked down by the rest of the nation.

Round goes to: *Dead heat.*

Tiebreaker—The TV Toss

In America we have freedom of speech. And what better way to voice your disgust and rage than to hurl your empty at the offending television? Here the advantage overwhelmingly goes to the can. With an empty beer can in his hand, the voiceless American TV viewer becomes like Elvis with a .38, blowing away the tube of any TV that pissed him off. If you've never taken the time to throw an empty at a TV, you owe it to yourself to experience one of life's simplest joys. It's like throwing rotten fruit at a bad singer . . . only it's an empty beer can and the State of the Union address.

Throw a bottle at the TV? You'd get a shower of glass that, even if it doesn't break the TV, shatters all over the floor. Nice going, dummy. Now making you have to wear *shoes* when you get off the couch to change the channel. Let's be honest, if you had a remote, you would have just changed the channel to begin with.

The Decision: *Can wins.*

However, if you're watching the TV at a *bar,* and you're planning on never coming back anyway . . .

LIGHT BEER V. DARK BEER

The light beer/dark beer debate—it's a quandary that has vexed mankind going all the way back to the 1970s.

Here's the deal. Ready? All light beers *suck.* There, I've said it. They're all bad, watered down versions of the real thing. Light beer has one purpose: To keep our women from getting fat. But why do guys drink it? Well, it's kind of like what happened with milk . . .

You started out getting delicious, whole-fat milk right from your mother's loving breast. Nothing could be more nourishing. So, like any guy, you ride that train as long as she'll let you. But as some men approach college age, they apparently stop *nursing* and start *counting calories.* They cut back on the blessed, white gazonga gravy, going from whole-fat to low fat, to 2% and finally the dreaded, tasteless nonfat. Eventually they've got nothing left to pour on their Cocoa Puffs but a cloudy milk-water. Pathetic.

Everyone knows at least one guy who cares more about his appearance than the taste of his beer. And while we all know that such a "man" can never be trusted, at least the silvery label on his brew makes him easy to spot. Let's face it, those "light beer" guys and their "abs" are a definite buzz kill.

The jolly beer gut was once considered an achievement—proof of one's fulfilling the American Dream. But the growing "light beer" faction is trying to turn your tubby testament to a life of luxury into some nonsense about you being "out of shape" or "dangerously close to a heart attack."

Truth be told, that bottle of light suds is a "gateway" beer to the more sinister stuff, low-carb and no-carb beers. Of course, the only reason for a guy to drink no-carb beer is because it doesn't stain when he spills it on his dress.

THE 40:
IT'S NOT JUST FOR BLACK GUYS ANYMORE

Malt liquor is essentially an extra-strong American light lager. Also, in some parts of the United States, any beer over a certain strength must legally be called "malt liquor." It's a "bang for your buck" drink that for years has mainly been marketed toward, and favored by, African Americans.

At more than 7.5% alcohol, malt liquor is to beer what fortified wine is to Kendall-Jackson. Crap. But crap that will put wings on your feet. Whether it's St. Ides, Olde English, Schlitz, or the holy mother of them all, Colt 45, this stuff has one purpose—to knock you on your ass and fuck your girlfriend.

Maybe it's a result of marketing, or maybe there's something cultural going on, but white guys have traditionally not been big buyers of malt liquor. Instead, they'll have a few beers after work, to relax or whatever. But black guys drink malt liquor to get the party started. Let's not bullshit each other. For years, the only white guys who drank this stuff were suburban teens who didn't know that drinking a six-pack of Olde English talls would make them wake up the next day in a puddle of their own piss.

But with hip-hop supplanting rock-'n'-roll as the predominant soundtrack to our cultural demise, something has happened to malt liquor. Its endless appearance in rap videos has made the mythical "40" a cool thing for white guys in search of an identity to latch on to.

The cultural divide was finally bridged when *drinking* malt liquor was made secondary to *spraying* it on a hot video vixen. Here at last, whites and blacks could move one step closer to Martin Luther King's dream. You no longer have to drink this swill to enjoy it. Because white or black, we all love wet tits.

LIGHT OF MY LIFE

There comes a time in any avid beer drinker's life that he must decide: "What's the right lighted beer sign for my basement?"

Well, that really depends. Is this basement the slowly evolving fulfillment of your lifelong dream to have your very own bar—with a real keg, fancy coasters, and a pinball machine—in your home? Or is this basement just the place where you'll sleep until your parents die and you finally get the house?

Well sir, if your basement is the former, then only one lighted beer sign will do: Hamm's.

The best Hamm's beer signs paid homage to the great outdoors—like a Schmidt's beer can. But unlike the Schmidt's can, which might feature a hunter's wet dream of elk in the woods or pheasants taking wing, the greatest Hamm's beer signs had a backlit wildlife scene with water that flowed for eternity, thanks to a motorized scroll of "water."

For generations Men have sat drinking in local joints, mesmerized by never-ending frosty mountain streams flowing into eternity, thanks to that gently cycling, endless scroll. The sign's soft azure glow forever beckons Men to the land of sky blue waters, a mythic place that exists somewhere beyond the smoky tavern, where we saw our first Hamm's beer sign, and beyond the oasis of our own lovingly converted basement bars.

But if your basement is simply where you're bunking down till your parents croak and you sell everything off before your siblings come around, then just stick with the cheerleader poster you've already put on the wall. Because even *you* can't jack off to a beer sign.

BEER THIRTY

There are as many beers out there as there are ways to enjoy them. Below are some of the many reasons you might want to guzzle a beer.

You're thirsty.

Because it's hot out.

You love the taste.

To make it easier to talk to women.

Your buddy's buying.

To go with your pizza.

To celebrate closing a big deal.

You've just roped your first steer.

You've just made your first bust.

To try to fit in at the company picnic.

You've just lost your virginity.

It's on sale.

You need courage.

You need a reward.

Your team won.

Your team lost.

Because you don't give a shit about sports.

You want to get drunk.

You got dumped.

You got fired.

Because you're still standing.

Because drinking Windex gives you a tummyache.

Because that asshole over there keeps glaring at you.

You really dig urinating.

Because all women are crazy (or "stupid," "evil," etc.).

Because empties are easier to hide from the wife.

You want to have some vomit for the sidewalk-painting contest later that night.

Because Jimi's still up there jammin' in heaven.

Because tonight, anyone who has ever wronged you will taste your revenge.

Because the cops are right behind you.

It helps wash down the pills.

Because it stops the voices.

You've just killed your cellmate.

You need to sign your name in some snow.

You've just gotten a tattoo that reads "Mother" . . . on your penis.

Because you're with friends.

FASHION

A few words about Beer and Fashion:

Generally, mixing anything "beer" with your attire is a "don't." Sure, that beer logo looks great on the many bottles and cans you've got piled out behind the trailer, but that doesn't mean you need to be a billboard for your brand. Unless you drive the big semi that brings the precious brew to the Safeway, you shouldn't wear the logo on your body. That's why a guy who's rockin' the Miller High Life trucker cap is really no cooler than the guy who's sporting a tiny wet spot of his favorite beer's remnants on the crotch of his pants.

But some guys have a love for beer and a complete lack of irony that compels them to sport their favorite brand of suds on their clothes. They just can't get enough of Stroh's T-shirts and Busch hats. Incidentally, it has been scientifically proven that any guy who wears two or more pieces of beer-related clothing will have mysterious stains on at least one of them.

Yet a strange phenomenon happens when those very same clothes are worn on a chick. Suddenly those cheesy vestments take on a whole new dimension. They're hot! Something about a cute girl in a goofy knit hat made out of Old Style cans, who's wearing a pair of tiny cut-offs held up by a Buckhorn belt buckle, screams "vixen." She's the one who at some point during the concert is going to be on a guy's shoulders with her top off, cheering the band on with her hands in the air while her perfect tits bounce to the beat of the drums.

Too bad she's with that dipshit in the Budweiser T-shirt.

THE BEER LOVER'S HAT

There isn't a child over the age of six who doesn't know that the hardhat with two beer cans strapped to the sides is the pinnacle of American beerphilia.

If you think about it, unless you're bald or it's raining out, there's no real reason to wear a hat in the summertime. But American ingenuity and mastery of technology has at last created headwear with a purpose—to double your intake of an intoxicant. It's just the kind of thing you might hear about in a beer-related death . . . and it makes a great gift.

Though everyone has seen the double-barreled beer hat, most guys don't have the balls to actually wear one. It takes a rare breed of Man to pull that off. You know the type. He's a dignified, go-his-own-way kind of guy who says, "Fuck it!" a lot. You'll usually find him dancing shirtless in the circle track bleachers, as the sun scorches his budding breasts.

A self-appointed mascot, he entertains the crowd. "I got a head on my beer, and beer on my head!" he repeatedly bellows. Later, his quip will become an unintelligible sputter interspersed with hiccups that dangerously approach vomiting, but it will still be every bit as funny to him.

Sometime around the third race he pulls out all the stops, slipping on a cardboard tray soaked with leftover ketchup and falling, teeth first, into the railing. And yes, some people laugh. The rest simply cheer.

And when the race is over, he heads back to his pickup with the picture of Calvin pissing on a Ford logo in the rear window. But this beer-swilling showman's work is never done. He's going out to a dinner tonight, which means a stop by the house for his "Pull My Finger" tank top.

MAN-O-VATION:
DISABILITY BEER HAT

Although everyone's seen the novelty beer hat with two cans of beer strapped to the sides, you may not be familiar with the Disability Beer Hat for men with no arms, the only beer-assist hat sanctioned by Medicare.

There are men all over who, through no fault of their own, have no arms. Some lost them fighting for this country, some lost them in industrial accidents, while others lost them when Green Bay didn't cover the spread. But these men need beer too. And this is the hat that gets the job done. It's constructed almost exactly like the novelty hat but uses American Medical Association (AMA) approved Velcro straps and surgical tubing, rather than cheap plastic or PVC.

For only $480, and the additional cost of one outpatient appointment for a fitting, most insurance companies and the VA will cover up to 85 percent of the cost.

If you know a man with no arms, reach out to him and let him know about the Disability Beer Hat.

* Also available: a model that works for men with arms but no hands. *

"DUDE . . . *THAT'S* MY BRAND"

There are men out there who develop a profound loyalty to their beer. Like a baseball team, a TV show, or any cult that's worth a shit, certain brands of beer have legions of devoted followers. They're the "that's my brand" faithful who can be counted on to offer colorful testimonials such as, "Nothing else will do," or "I'd rather go without than switch . . . and *that's* why it's in my truck, Officer."

Loyalty comes in many stripes. There are Coors drinkers. Bud drinkers. PBR guys who've been drinking it for thirty years. I'm a huge believer in having a total, unequivocal loyalty to one brand . . . I've had it several times.

Why do guys have brand loyalty? Because loyalty gives guys a sense of "belonging." This quasi-religious sense of team spirit bonds men, making it possible to build civilizations, raise the flag at Iwo Jima, and play "who farted?" for an entire three-day camping trip. Beer loyalty is all about belonging to something—and not something phony like a gym. These guys would never stoop so low as to belong to evil gyms, with their unholy high prices, their blasphemous one-year-no-money-back commitment, and their fucking ab crunchers.

Similar to religion, brand loyalty gives some folks both comfort and support through life's troublesome times. They've seen the power of their loyalty, for it moves in mysterious ways. Like when they're so smashed they can barely speak, yet their brand's name is the one word their bartender can still make out.

Brand loyalty can be determined by a lot of things: price, availability, and price. It's certainly not because of *taste*. There's nothing remotely tasteful about the homeless guy who's halfway through a twelve-pack of Old Milwaukee piss. The closest he could come to "taste" is to finish the rest of them and barf you a Jackson Pollack. He bought that cheap swill for the same reason you bought it in college, because he could afford it. He's not homeless, he's frat-houseless. His brand of loyalty was determined by cost.

But there are times when brand loyalty can be shortsighted. Before you swear your life over to MGD or Bud, remember all those guys out there who once pledged their allegiance to Blatz beer. They're like Brooklyn after the Dodgers left for Los Angeles. The town was never the same after it lost its beloved team. Like no town ever had, Brooklyn loved their "bums" who rode the subway and broke the color barrier with Jackie Robinson. And still the Dodgers left—forever. Slow death.

So, in the words of another Robinson, Smokey, "You better shop around." Next time you're out having a beer at a bar, picking up a six-pack or stealing a keg, grab just *one* bottle of something you've never tried before. Because, trite as it seems, beers are like women. You owe it to yourself to experience as many as you can before you decide on "the One."

Here's another reason. Are you ready? You should hold off on claiming a brand loyalty because it could be, it just might be—if there's a God in Heaven—it just *might* be that you're the lucky son of a bitch who, like Hefner, Casanova, or the non-white players in the NBA, never, *ever* has to settle on just one.

With beer, we have the best odds of being perpetual playboys, going from one sweet, young, brand-new beer to another—no questions asked.

We are Men because we dare to dream.

Sadly, corporate brewers, the Church, and your woman have prevented you from becoming the Mack Daddy of beer.

You are not the Chosen One.

YOU'VE FOUND YOUR BEER WHEN . . .

Finding the right brand to remain loyal to can be difficult. Some romantics will say, "Don't worry, you'll just know." Well, the rest of us can't be so sure. This list will help you determine if you've found the beer you'll be with for the rest of your life.

You've found your beer when:

You come home every night and it's waiting for you.

You can spend hours with it and not even notice the time.

You don't have to work very hard to get its top off.

It doesn't mind you spending your time together sitting on the couch, watching TV.

Its "born on" date doesn't go back too far.

Even though you know maybe hundreds of other guys have had it, you can't stop going back to it.

It doesn't break your balls if you haven't seen it all weekend.

It doesn't matter if it's light or dark, color is no longer important.

It doesn't bother you while you're taking a shit.

It doesn't fuck with your head while you're trying to drive.

You wake up in the morning and it's there, right next to you, spread out on your sheets.

And finally, you know you're going to be with that beer for the rest of your life when . . . it says, "I'm pregnant."

YOU'VE GOT QUESTIONS, BEER HAS ANSWERS

As you may have guessed,

this section is dedicated to providing useful, everyday information about beer. Plus it's got hot chicks in it. Since this will be the most thumbed section of the book, it will answer some of the most commonly asked questions, except for, "Are those real?"

Crystal Colar, Vanessa Kay, Angelique Gorges, Christie Hemme (top of stairs), Lisa Ligon, Kathryn Smith

FAQS

O kay, here's the thing about Frequently Asked Questions: You could've gotten these answers for *free* off the Web, ass clown. Maybe the first question you *should* have asked is, "Gee, what *else* can I do with this Internet thing besides search for porno and pictures of my ex-girlfriend at her office party?" But since you've paid for the book, the Juggies will answer your FAQs (with a little help when needed).

What is beer?

KATHIE: *"If I remember correctly, beer was $4.75 . . . but if you wanted to do a Purple Hooter or Fuzzy Navel from my test-tube belt, it was six bucks."*

Actually, beer is an alcoholic beverage made from malted grains, hops, yeast, and water. The grain is usually barley or wheat. Fruit, herbs, and spices may also be used for special styles. In the distant past, the terms "beer" and "ale" meant different things. Unlike beer, ale was originally made without hops. Since most commercial brews now use hops, the term "beer" now encompasses two broad categories: ales and lagers.

What is a "dry beer"?

VANESSA: *"Huh? How can a beer be dry? You wouldn't be able to see my boobs through the T-shirt. How stupid!"*

Dry beer was developed by Japanese brewers by using more adjuncts (like corn and rice) and genetically altered yeasts. Dry beers ferment more completely and have less residual sweetness, and hence less aftertaste.

What does it mean when a beer is "heat pasteurized"?

LISA: *"Actually, 'heat pasteurized' is a redundant phrase since pasteurization means heating to kill microbes. Anyway, some beers are bottle or cask conditioned, which means that there's live yeast still in the beer. But most mainstream beers are either filtered to remove all yeast and bacteria, or pasteurized to kill all yeast and bacteria. This process makes for a product with a longer shelf life. . . . I used to sleep with an executive vice president for West Coast distribution at Anheuser-Busch."*

. . . as well as several of the Portland Trailblazers.

Why is "beer piss" sometimes clear?

ANGELIQUE: *"It is? No way! I didn't know that! C'mon, we're Juggies, we don't pee!"*

The Church says clear pee is God's way of protecting the seat when you pass out on the plane.

What is bock beer?

CHRISTIE: *"Bock beer? Ya got me. If I had a boyfriend, I'd ask him, but lately, I've been into chicks."*

Bock beer was traditionally brewed in Germany during the fall, which is the end of the growing season, when barley and hops were at their peak. Bock beer is "lagered" all winter and enjoyed in the spring at the beginning of the new brewing season.

Why does my beer sometimes smell skunky?

CRYSTAL: *"Maybe you just need to wash it more."*

Beer smells skunky because it has spoiled. When beer is exposed to certain wavelengths of natural or artificial light, photochemical reactions in the hop resins result in a sulfury mercaptan, which has a pronounced skunky smell. To prevent this from happening, beer usually comes in a brown bottle.

TEN THINGS YOU DIDN'T KNOW ABOUT BEER

1. Unlike wine, beer should be stored upright so that the cap doesn't rust and taint the bottle's contents. . . . The only time it's okay to put beer on its side is while you're cramming it under your seat as the cops are pulling you over.

2. The Bavarian Purity Law of 1516, or *Reinheitsgebot* (*Rein* means "pure"; *Gebot* means "commandment") says only four legitimate ingredients are allowed in beer: water, barley, hops, and yeast. . . . So yeah, you were right, that cigarette butt wasn't supposed to be in there.

3. Oktoberfest actually begins in the third week of September. . . . This is done so it can coincide with Beerpissundsausagediarrheafest.

4. The average American annually consumes 23.1 gallons of beer . . . but it takes him nearly 365 days to do it.

5. It takes more than thirty days to brew a Budweiser . . . but *you* can turn water into piss in under an hour.

6. Twelve ounces of a typical American pale lager actually have fewer calories than 2% milk or apple juice . . . and just *slightly* more alcohol.

7. The first beer cans were produced in 1935. . . . At the time the invention was hailed as "the greatest thing," and as a result put a lot of sliced bread out of work.

8. Most brewers agree that the fastest way to destroy a beer's flavor is to expose it to sunlight. . . . The second fastest way is to expose it to your kidneys.

9. A typical 12-ounce beer contains no fat and fewer calories than two slices of bread. . . . However, once it's in the toaster, its limitations become obvious.

10. Anthropologists estimate that beer first appeared about ten thousand years ago, but it took another two thousand years before wine showed up. . . . Apparently the guy had to go to like six places before his fake ID worked.

HANGOVER CURES

B e warned, a lot of this stuff is from that font of spurious information, the Internet, which means it may have just as much validity as the "we never landed on the moon" crap.

The hair of the dog: It can work, somewhat. Alcohol is a painkiller of sorts, and isn't that why you were drinking in the first place?

Sweat it out: Makes sense, as long as you drink plenty of water. Your body's metabolism will kick in to process the alcohol, and you'll get rid of toxins in your sweat. You could get up and do forty-five minutes on the orbital trainer . . . or just crank up the heater and stay under the covers.

Large greasy breakfast: This is a great idea even when you're not hungover. The theory is that because alcohol is fat soluble, it will be absorbed by the grease and will only pass through your stomach lining and into your bloodstream with the rate at which you digest food. This *can* help slow down the rate at which you get drunk, but by the time you're feeling the crush of a hangover, it's too late for greasy food. That alcohol was in your bloodstream hours ago. But don't let that stop you from enjoying your bacon.

Juices: The water in juice rehydrates your body, the fructose (sugar) it contains helps burn up the alcohol.

Eat grains: Eat rice, grains, cereals, peas, and nuts. They're jammed full of vitamin B1, or thiamine, which helps you metabolize the alcohol and stabilizes your shattered nerves. Lack of B1 is supposedly what causes the infamous delirium tremens, better known as "the shakes."

V8 Juice: Well, it couldn't hurt. It's wet, and is made of stuff that at one time had nutritional value. You might as well get the spicy kind, unless your stomach is too much of a pussy.

Kudzu: Kudzu is a Chinese vine that, legend has it, was used to cure hangovers as early as 200 BC. According to a white person that I met, who I seriously doubt speaks Chinese, kudzu was recommended as a hangover cure in the *Chinese Pharmacopoeia* around 400 AD. So it's probably about as effective as all that stuff that the Chinese claim will give you bionic boners.

Rose Oil: The theory is that a drop of rose oil on the temples dilates your capillaries and boosts the blood flow to your brain. An even better way to increase blood flow to the head is to bend over. You'll feel loaded all over again, which is better than feeling hungover.

Ginseng: According to some guy on the Internet, ginseng is supposedly a favorite of Canadian loggers who drink all night and still get to knocking down birds' nests come sunrise. The preferred dosage is 500mg of ginseng (liquid or pill form) first thing in the morning with a Red Bull chaser. Because when you're sleep deprived, hungover, and jacked up on Red Bull, the first thing you want to do is fire up a chainsaw.

HANGOVER SMOOTHIE

Stumble around and find:

1 banana
1 pint of milk
honey

Cut up the banana and mix it in a blender with the milk . . . because nothing soothes nerves shattered by alcohol abuse like the grinding roar of a blender. Add a couple generous spoonfuls of honey and blend into a shake.

The science: *The milk is supposed to settle your stomach. The honey will provide the necessary sugars to give you a boost. The banana will release sugars at a sustained rate to keep you up after the honey's effect has faded.*

Does it cure a hangover? Who knows? But if you throw some rum in there, you might have something.

SOME LIKE IT HOT

We've all heard of places where they drink warm beer—a frightful proposition to most Americans. But when you take away their weird accents, bad clothes, grinding poverty, and funny music, foreigners love beer and drinking as much as we do.

"The mouth of a perfectly happy man is filled with beer."
—EGYPTIAN INSCRIPTION, 2200 BC

"When the bee comes to your house, let her have beer; you may want to visit the bee's house some day."
—CONGOLESE PROVERB

"It takes beer to make thirst worthwhile."
—GERMAN SAYING

"A fine beer may be judged with only one sip, but it's better to be thoroughly sure."
—CZECH PROVERB

"Man's way to God is with beer in hand."
—NIGERIAN PROVERB

"May Ninkasi (Goddess of beer) live with you. Let her pour your beer everlasting."
—ANCIENT SUMERIAN BLESSING

"The church is near, but the road is icy. The bar is far away, but I will walk carefully."
—OLD RUSSIAN PROVERB

"In wine there is wisdom, in beer there is strength, in water there is bacteria."
—GERMAN PROVERB

"Froth is not beer."
—DUTCH PROVERB

"Drinking is what makes a man shoot at his landlord . . . and what makes him miss."
—IRISH PROVERB

"They speak of my drinking, but never of my thirst."
—SCOTTISH PROVERB

WHITHER SPUDS?

People often wonder, what ever happened to Spuds McKenzie?

Some people say that Spuds McKenzie was actually played by *three* dogs. The two males were from the same well-known sire, the third, a female, from an independent breeder. The company line is that Spuds was dropped because it was time for change. Apparently focus groups showed that after two and a half years of watching a dog live out their dreams, consumers were now seeking a more "human" quality to their brand-related "buddy". . . and Spuds terrified children under three.

Others wryly joke that Spuds quietly lived out his last years at the Anheuser-Busch home for retired Budweiser mascots until he was trampled to death one day by a drunk Clydesdale—which finally opened up a room for the very patient Ed McMahon.

But others, Spuds's *real* fans, the people whom he spoke for, they know the sad truth. They tell the tale of how their hero, Spuds, died one day at a pool party at Larry Flynt's. "Spuds was walking to the diving board and gonna do another totally rad cannonball, but he got distracted by this smokin' hot centerfold chick with giant tits. And when he wasn't looking, he was accidentally run over by Larry's wheelchair. There was nothing they could do, man. He died immediately, like Kurt. Take it easy, man. I know it's fucked up, but take it easy. It's okay because when they rolled that crippled dude's chair offa Spuds? He had a frosty cold *Bud* in his paw. . . . Fuckin' Spuds, man! Right on!"

Whither Spuds? He's partying with Janis and Jimi.

JINGLES

Back in the day, even crappy beers could have pretty good jingles. Whether you heard them listening to the ball game on the radio or watched their commercials on TV, they stuck in your head.

Name the beers whose jingles and slogans had these famous lines:

1. **"Here's to good friends . . ."**

2. **"What'll you have? . . ."**

3. **"When it's time to relax . . ."**

4. **"Look out for the bull . . ."**

5. **"Here comes the king . . ."**

6. **"From the land of sky blue waters . . ."**

7. **"_____ is the one beer to have, when you're having more than one."**

8. **"When you're out of _____, you're out of beer."**

9. **"When you say _____, you've said it all."**

10. **"I'd like to buy the world a . . ."**

ANSWERS: 1 Lowenbrau; **2** Pabst Blue Ribbon; **3** Miller; **4** Schlitz Malt Liquor; **5** Budweiser; **6** Hamm's; **7** Schaeffer; **8** Schlitz; **9** Bud; **10** Surprisingly, not Budweiser. This song was an ad for Coke, the Budweiser of the soft drink world.

WAZZZUUUUPPP?

There've been many unforgettable beer ad campaigns over the years on TV. Anyone over thirty remembers Miller Lite's "Less Filling/Tastes Great" spots that introduced America to the whole concept of "light" beer. Today, that same battle rages on in poolside catfights.

Do you remember the "Artesians" from the Olympia commercials? How about the Schlitz Malt Liquor Bull, and the Swedish Ski Team? Who could forget the "Now comes Miller Time," or the "Tonight, let it be Lowenbrau" spots? A memorable commercial can boost the sales of even the crappiest of beers.

The company that reigns supreme in ad campaigns has got to be Anheuser-Busch, makers of Budweiser. Among the many pop culture touchstones they've brought you are the Budweiser frogs, Spuds McKenzie, the Clydesdales, the Bud Bowl, and the freakish red-headed Delivery Guy who ran around trying to keep Bud from going skunky.

Sometimes the ads are so successful, they serve a purpose other than making you aware of a beer product. Which brings us to the "Wazzzuuuuppp!" commercials from a couple of years ago. For some, this whole ad campaign was a godsend, because if ever there was a word that became the quickest way to find out if someone was a dildo, it was "Wazzzuuuuppp!"

What an incredible timesaver. Anytime I heard someone say "Wazzzuuuuppp!" with anything other than retarded irony, I knew right away he was someone I didn't really need to talk to. This word alone could save me the two minutes it would have taken him before he said some other telltale line like "I gotta drink light beer because when I was at a party the other night, I took my shirt off and I realized it's time to get my chest waxed again." See? A dildo.

Thank you, Budweiser.

A FEW WORDS ABOUT BEER

Here's a collection of great quotes about beer and drinking.

"He was a wise man who invented beer."
—PLATO

"I'm allergic to grass. Hey, it could be worse. I could be allergic to beer."
—GREG NORMAN

"Thought of giving it all away, to a registered charity. All I need is a pint a day."
—PAUL McCARTNEY

KIRK: *"Romulan ale . . . Why, Bones, you know this is illegal."*
McCOY: *"I only use it for medicinal purposes."*
—*STAR TREK II: THE WRATH OF KHAN*

"You can't be a real country unless you have a beer and an airline.
It helps if you have some kind of a football team or some nuclear weapons,
but at the very least, you need a beer."
—FRANK ZAPPA

"Beer is proof that God loves us."
—BENJAMIN FRANKLIN

"Buy a man a beer, and he wastes an hour.
Teach a man to brew, and he wastes a lifetime."
—BILL OWENS, EDITOR, *AMERICAN BREWER*

"I think this would be a good time for a beer."
—FRANKLIN D. ROOSEVELT
(upon signing his New Deal legislation paving the way for the repeal of Prohibition)

"Twenty-four hours in a day, twenty-four beers in a case. Coincidence?"
—STEVEN WRIGHT

"All right, brain: I don't like you, and you don't like me.
So let's just do this, and I'll get back to killing you with beer."
—HOMER J. SIMPSON

"A quart of ale is a dish fit for a king."
—WILLIAM SHAKESPEARE

"If you ever reach total enlightenment while drinking beer,
I bet it makes beer shoot out your nose."
—JACK HANDEY, *DEEP THOUGHTS*

"Ah, good ol' trustworthy beer. My love for you will never die."
—HOMER J. SIMPSON

"The problem with the world is that everyone is a few drinks behind."
—HUMPHREY BOGART

"Why is American beer served cold? So you can tell it from urine."
—DAVID MOULTON

"People who drink light 'beer' don't like the taste of beer;
they just like to pee a lot."
—CAPITAL BREWERY, MIDDLETON, WI

"When I first read about the evils of drinking, I gave up reading."
—HENNY YOUNGMAN

"Time is never wasted when you're wasted all the time."
—CATHERINE ZANDONELLA

"You're not drunk if you can lie on the floor without holding on."
—DEAN MARTIN

*"You can only drink thirty or forty glasses of beer a day,
no matter how rich you are."*
—COLONEL ADOLPHUS BUSCH

"They who drink beer will think beer."
—WASHINGTON IRVING

*"It only takes one drink to get me drunk.
The problem is I can never remember if it is the twelfth or thirteenth."*
—GEORGE BURNS

*"'Twas a woman who drove me to drink,
and I never had the courtesy to thank her for it."*
—W. C. FIELDS

*"I feel sorry for people who don't drink. When they wake up in the morning,
that's as good as they're going to feel all day."*
—FRANK SINATRA

"Sometimes too much drink is barely enough."
—MARK TWAIN

*"I decided to stop drinking with creeps. I decided to drink only with friends.
I've lost thirty pounds."*
—ERNEST HEMINGWAY

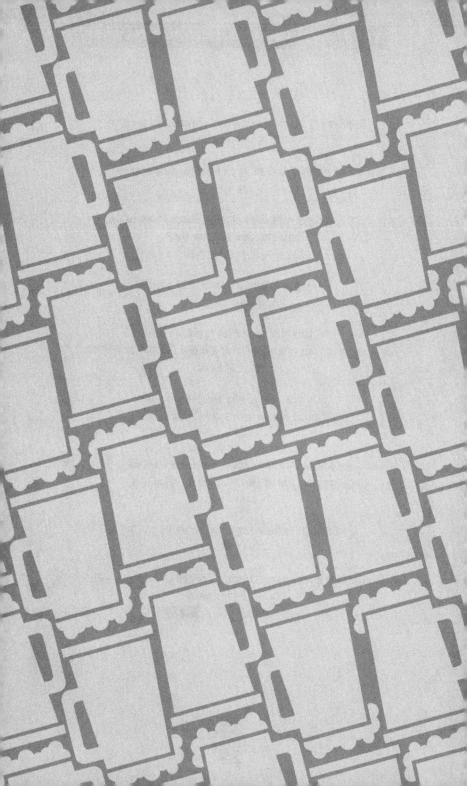

SHOW ME THE WAY

It's not always the case

that Man seeks answers because he needs a problem solved. Sometimes he seeks knowledge and wisdom for their own sake. Just as the quest to understand how our vast universe works is one of the noblest of endeavors, so it is for the smaller universe of beer. The answers to the great questions in this realm are now presented for your enlightenment.

HOW TO SHOTGUN A BEER

S hotgunning a beer is probably the greatest thing since . . . uh . . . canned beer. Is there a purpose to shotgunning a beer? Not really. It may make you drink faster than you would have, had you simply tried to chug it, but mostly shotgunning is a cool way to gulp suds with your buds. It's a bonding ritual. Oh sure, there are occasions when a guy will shotgun a beer when he's all alone . . . and cleaning his knife . . . vowing revenge. . . . But the rest of us, we'll only shotgun a can of beer at a party, or when we're with at least one friend, vowing revenge.

Here's how it's done.

Do not shake the can, unless you *want* a beer shower. Simply punch a hole near the bottom of the can on the side. You'd be surprised how easily that aluminum can will puncture. Anything will do—a screwdriver, a nail file, the pointy end of a bottle opener. Maybe that weirdo from the previous paragraph will lend you his knife. Just be careful. Once punctured, the can may have sharp edges exposed. The only place beer and blood go together is in a domestic violence dispute.

Put your mouth over the hole you've made; tilt your head and the can upright. Now pull the tab and start swallowing. If you spill any beer, you're a punk. Seconds later, you'll find you've got 12 ounces of frothy fun in your gut. Good times. Now, see that girl standing over by the stereo? Get her to do one. Those pants aren't going to come off by themselves.

HOW TO OPEN A BEER WITH A LIGHTER

This is a handy skill for when you've graduated to beers that don't have a "twist-off." There's going to come that time when you don't have a church key and you don't have a car bumper or any furniture nearby. Most likely you're outdoors, and let's face it, unemployed. But that doesn't have to stop you from enjoying yourself. Get out

Figure 1

Figure 2

Figure 3

Figure 4

your Bic lighter, or for you nonsmokers, your lighter-sized object, and follow these instructions. You're going to use one of Man's oldest tools, the lever, to free that beer from the bottle.

1. Grasp the bottle around the neck, with the top of your fist just about even with the *top* of the bottle cap. Extend your index finger, while holding on to the bottle with however many fingers you have left on that hand. Just *don't* use your index finger to hold the bottle, because you're going to need that for step 3.

2. Place the base of the lighter so that it "stands up" on your middle finger.

3. Now wrap your index finger around the lighter and squeeze it tightly against the bottle. The lighter is now a "lever" and your index finger is the "fulcrum."

4. Place the thumb of that hand over the top of the cap.

5. With your other hand, use an overhand grip to take hold of the top of the lighter.

6. Keeping a tight grip that squeezes the bottom of the lighter against the bottle, use your other hand to push the top of the lighter downward and away from you.

7. Drink.

Unlike flicking the bottle cap (discussed later in this chapter), you should have gotten this one on the first try. But there's always a chance you're a moron. However, if you've succeeded, you're ready to be the hero who saves the day and opens the beer while everyone else is standing around waiting to drink. And best of all, this little maneuver is a great way to impress a lady . . . if she's the kind of lady who was raised in a cave or dungeon with no human contact.

HOW TO OPEN A BEER WITH YOUR TEETH

First of all, DON'T! Isn't there a fence post or a guy with a *lighter* around? How badly do you *need* this beer, anyway? Maybe it's time to reexamine your drinking habits, because chancing a broken tooth and an exposed nerve for a swig of Keystone lager does not speak well of your risk assessment capabilities.

Before you go down this route, take a moment to think about just exactly *who* opens bottles with their teeth: carny folk, convicts, Uzbeks, and grannies on TV shows featuring colorful hillbillies. Now, if you're a member of one of those groups and you're just in need of a little advice to get you on your way to full-fledged scarydom, then fine, I apologize. But if you're not, I must inform you that the danger of this "talent" is so great that you should get a *buddy* to try this instead.

1. Hold the bottle in your hands and place your lower front teeth under the cap as close to the glass as you can.

2. Place your upper teeth on the top of the cap somewhere past the middle point. The key here is that you're going to use this leverage to bend the cap so that it will come off.

3. Clench your jaw tight to hold the cap firmly as you use steady pressure from the wrists to push the bottom of the bottle away from you.

4. Either continue pushing until the cap pops off and proceed to Step 5, or punk out, turn in your keys to the Tilt-A-Whirl, and remove the bent cap with your hand.

5. Say good-bye to that tooth enamel and hello to a life on the road, one step ahead of the law.

Thanks to Ian Miller from Queens, New York

HOW TO OPEN A BEER WITH YOUR EYE

Yep, you read right. Opening a bottle in your eye socket seems like the sort of thing one might do in college, but guys who do this usually bypass college and go straight to the steel mill or coal mine and never see the light of day again. The truth is, if you're the type who would ever even *think* of opening a bottle with your eye socket, you've probably already done so. You're not *made,* you're *born.* You test the sharpness of a knife by licking it and get aroused at the sight of burning buildings. So you, and anybody who bleeds a lot when they shave, can move on to the next page.

For the rest of you, before you attempt this, there are a couple of things you need to consider: Will I really be able to fall asleep at night if I have no eyelids? And how will I explain the black eye to my parole officer? Okay, here's how it's done:

1. Make sure your wife, girlfriend, mother, or any other sensible person isn't home.

2. Take a bottle of beer—a twist-off, please—and hold it up to your closed eye. Use whichever eye you don't really need or the one that will look coolest with a patch.

3. Seat the cap firmly against the highest part of your cheekbone and the top of your eye socket.

4. Close your eye as hard as you can and twist the bottle clockwise. If you've gotten enough of your skin wrapped around the cap, it should absorb the pressure and twist it off.

If you're the beady-eyed type with a big brow ridge, this is probably your lucky day. If not, keep trying. Until you get enough calluses under your eyelid, you can count on some cheek abrasions, but they'll probably match your knuckles.

HOW TO OPEN A BEER WITH YOUR BUTT

Apparently this method of opening a beer bottle is used in parts of rural Kentucky. It gets a laugh, and if you stick to only using this technique to open beers for your girlfriend, it'll take the whole "I'm-jamming-something-up-my-ass" homoerotic vibe off it . . . almost.

1. Take a bottle of beer and cram it as deep between your ass cheeks as your pants will allow. My guess is a long-neck works best.

2. Squeeze your cheeks tight to grab hold of the cap, and using a combination of twisting and shoving harder into your ass, your pants should cause enough friction and resistance to torque the cap off the bottle.

3. It may help if you try to think of the bottle cap as a "nut" and your butt as a damp, sweaty, smelly "socket." Maybe you already do.

HOW TO BREAK YOUR BUDDY'S FINGER

Actually, when done properly, this scam will have him breaking his own finger. **THE SETTING:**: You and your buddy at your home, or in your El Camino in front of your ex-girlfriend's house, or behind the stack of boxes at work, or wherever else you and your friend drink together.

YOU'LL NEED: A couple of six-packs of Grolsch beer. If you aren't a fan of Dutch lagers, you're out of luck. It *has* to be Grolsch because this little trick requires its distinctive "swing top" cap.

THE ACTION: You and your buddy drink. Sometime after you've had a couple beers, you pick up another fresh bottle of Grolsch. Make sure your friend watches as you nonchalantly open it by whacking the top off the bottle with a pop from your finger.

It looks pretty impressive. He may ask you how you did it, or better still, he'll try to do the same with his next bottle, unsuccessfully. No matter how hard he tries, he will not be able to open the bottle the way he just saw you do it. If he asks you to do it again, you have to play it cool. Reseal your bottle and pop the top once more, stressing how easy it is. He will get frustrated each time he tries to open the bottle and will later have to ice down his hand.

HOW TO DO IT: The trick is all in how you position your striking hand. As you bring your hand forward toward the top of the bottle, let your thumb hang down so it can catch the lower part of the hinged wire that holds the lid on. Make sure that as you hit the top of the bottle (try using your middle finger and index finger in tandem for added stability), your thumb hits the bottom of the wire first. The combination of your thumb taking the pressure off the cap and the impact of your fingers will open the bottle fairly easily.

Practice it a couple of times before you mystify your buddy and then *NEVER* tell him how you do it. Have fun with it. Tell him that like a karate master smashing through bricks, he has to think "through" the cap as if it's not even there. Pop the lid off again as a demonstration. He'll never play piano again. Or at least won't jack off for a week.

HOW TO FLICK A BOTTLE CAP

What's cooler than casually taking the cap off your bottle and sending it on a bee-line across the room with just a snap of your fingers? Well, lots of stuff. Perhaps the question should have been, What can you do *with a bottle cap* that's cooler than zapping it around the room with deadly accuracy? That's what editing is for. Anyway, here's how you do it:

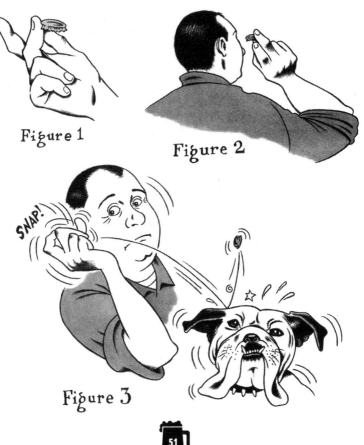

Figure 1

Figure 2

SNAP!

Figure 3

1. Open a bottle of beer.

2. Drink the contents.

3. Take the cap between your middle finger and your thumb. Let the cap rest on your thumb with your middle finger just barely gripping it on the side. The trick here is not to squeeze. (See Figure 1.)

4. Tuck your other fingers out of the way.

5. Raise your elbow to about 90 degrees so that your bottle cap is close to your ear. This will keep your cap from rocketing to the floor. (See Figure 2.)

6. Point your elbow in the direction you want the cap to fly.

7. Snap your fingers as hard as you can. (See Figure 3.)

8. That was pathetic. Get your head out of your ass. Look around behind you for the cap and go back and repeat steps 3 through 6.

9. This time don't think about the cap. Just snap *hard* and let your middle finger thrust the cap off its resting place, the thumb.

10. Okay, you're a slow learner. But it works if you practice.

With a couple more beers and a little more practice, you will move on to the final step, which is taking your buddy to the emergency room to see just how deeply you scarred his retina. (See figure 4.)

MAN-O-VATION:
NOTHING BUT NET CAN

You no longer have to suck at flicking your bottle caps. Your spastic attempts to flick a cap won't be an embarrassment anymore, because the Nothing But Net trash can ensures that every bottle cap makes a basket.

How does it work?

Amazing breakthroughs in product liability deregulation enable the Nothing But Net can to magically attract your errant bottle caps. The specially designed can uses powerful magnetic technologies that are so . . . *powerful,* that even if you accidentally *drop* a bottle cap, it's "Nothing But Net."

The Nothing But Net can comes with two enormous, synchronized diesel engines with a combined rating of over 23,000 horsepower to energize a massive electromagnet, engineered to generate a flux density of 10^{12} Gauss. That's enough to impose force on even the *biggest* bottle caps!*

Your power plant is housed in a handsome workshop, made from a kit that accompanies your Nothing But Net can that you construct behind your home. Providing a soothing hum at just under 84 decibels, this hungry monster only needs refueling once every 46 hours. That's nearly *three* times less than your dog!

So the next time you flick a cap, make it Nothing But Net!

* Wiring not included.

CAN I BUY YOU A DRINK?

It's no secret that

if it weren't for inebriation on someone's part, most of us wouldn't be here. For many, beer is an integral part of the courting process. It's there from the first night, when you eagerly bought her round after round in a transparent attempt to get down her pants, and it's there on the last, when you guzzle a parade of cheap beers after she dumps you for a guy with a better car (read: "bigger cock") and a job (read: "no criminal record").

But for now, let us look at happier times.

TEN REASONS WHY
A BEER IS BETTER THAN A WOMAN

1. If you wanted to, you could have them two at a time.

2. When a beer gets old, you can dump it.

3. You can pick up a beer without having to fake an interest in it.

4. It's never a problem getting a beer to go down.

5. Even Bud Dry is always wet.

6. Your beer doesn't mind you sharing it with a friend.

7. A beer bottle never loses its shape.

8. When you toss one out of a car, it's usually the last you'll ever see of it.

9. If at some point, you decide that you're just not into beer, no one calls you "homo."

10. When a beer goes through your pants, you have shame, but you still have your money.

BEER GOGGLES

Even if it's only for one night, both men and women have minimum requirements that they look for in a potential sex partner: a pretty face, a job, a nice rack, clean hands, consciousness, or at least three major limbs. But drinking too much beer can throw those standards out the window. Known as putting on "beer goggles," drinking yourself into a fog may cause you not to notice or dwell upon a potential mate's shortcomings.

You might look to the other end of the bar and see a fat girl with food on her shirt. But five to six beers later, it's bye-bye to the girl with the "great personality," hello to a vixen, ripe for an ass party. If she shoots you down, you just move on to her even more ugly friend. How did you miss *this* beauty who's been sitting there all night?

Donning beer goggles can also be a conscious decision. There are times when you want to get laid, but when you scope out the bar, you see only slim pickins. So you call out to the bartender, "Make mine a double."

Leading scientists have found that the relative thickness of the beer goggles is directly proportional to how late in the evening it is. The later the hour, the better the goggles are at filtering out someone's imperfections. By last call, your beer goggles may form a dark welder's mask that few things short of her having a penis bigger than yours can penetrate.

Aside from a lifetime of regret and the occasional murder, the only other downside to beer goggles is that they can wear off too early. Nothing is worse than hammering away on a girl that's even fatter and uglier than you, and suddenly losing your buzz. You don't want to cease the Hammering Process, because that would be rude, but staring at that messed-up mug can make it hard to maintain your focus. That's why I offer you this humble tip:

Always have a reliever twelve-pack to keep your goggles from "falling off." Worst-case scenario, you can always place the empty box over her head.

MAN-O-VATION:
MCB 5000

One problem with having "a few too many" while out on the town is that we could, in our intoxicated state, bring home a girl we're not going to want to wake up to. I'm not talking about the ones that are crazy, because as we all know, they're the ones we *want* to bring home for sex. Not even amputees, because even miss goody-one-shoe likes to get her freak on. We're talking about girls who weigh more than you do and the horror you experience after you take them home. If only there was some foolproof technology that could protect you from such a disaster again.

Well, now there is. . . .

Loosely based on the same car Breathalyzers that make it impossible to start your car if your blood alcohol is over the legal limit, the new Mobile Cock Block 5000 is guaranteed to make sure you never again wake up with Shamu.

Here's how it works:

Your car's ignition is rewired to the base of the Mobile Cock Block 5000, which is mounted on the passenger side of the dashboard. At the other end of the device is clamped a crispy piece of bacon. When you and the "Catch-of-the-Day" get in your car, you simply put the salty pork end of the Mobile Cock Block 5000 into her mouth for eight seconds. If it's gone when you pull it out, your car will not start, and she's walking home.

Thanks to the Mobile Cock Block 5000, the only sweaty, bloated body you'll wake up with will be your own.

SEX

While we're on the subject, a few words about drinking and sex.

As your wife or girlfriend can tell you, if it weren't for booze, most of us would never get laid. Booze makes you more confident, and her a lot less discerning. For many guys, getting her loaded is the only move they've got. However, if you're planning on getting some, it's best that you drink in moderation.

Why? Because you don't want to have a power failure at the crucial moment. Though it's never happened to this writer, it seems "too much sauce can make the meat too tender" if you know what I mean. No? Uh . . . "Too much, uh, *gas* will flood the *engine*"? Uh . . . Aw hell, you'll be too drunk to fuck, okay?

You'll have the girl there, waiting for a delivery of sizzling Mansteak and you're going to embarrass yourself, trying to get inside her with your gelatinous Johnson. You might as well try to pry open a pair of elevator doors with a Nerf bat.

But don't freak out and go into a homosexual panic. It's most likely this errant power failure doesn't mean you're gay. In fact, the only reliable test for gayness is if you have a *favorite* character on *Will & Grace.* No, you'll just sleep it off and live to fight another day. Way to go, Drinkie. Welcome to planet "She's Gonna Tell Her Friends."

But to avoid this problem in the future, you can consult this Beers-to-Boners chart. Notice that as the number of beers goes up, your rod goes down.

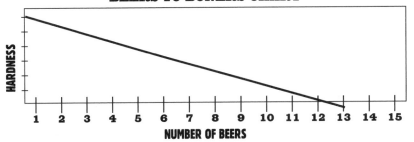

BEERS-TO-BONERS CHART

HARDNESS

NUMBER OF BEERS

1 2 3 4 5 6 7 8 9 10 11 12 13 14 15

AT ONE BEER . . . . .your rod is in great shape. He's rock hard and more than a little cocky.

BY BEER THREE . . . . .your boner is still hard, but it often becomes very indiscriminate. At this point it's actually fond of women with a lot of junk in the trunk.

AFTER FIVE OR . . . . .your member can start to get a little spongy, but it **SIX BEERS** makes up for that in belligerence. He may even leap out at people.

AFTER NINE OR . . . . .many wieners can barely stand up long enough to do **TEN BEERS** the job. Though the spirit is willing, the flesh becomes weak.

BY TWELVE OR . . . . .it's lights-out for most penii. It's drunk, squishy, and **THIRTEEN BEERS** usually passes out long before you do.

AT FIFTEEN BEERS . . . . .your penis is no longer a sexual organ. It's now a very unreliable barrier between your bladder and some fat girl's mattress. And once again, for the record, I want to stress that this has never happened to this writer.

CHOOSING A BEER FOR YOUR WEDDING

Whether you're getting married because you've realized she's the only one for you, or because you were drunk and the rubber broke, you should be consulted on which beer is served at the reception. This is the *only* decision you might have any say in . . . for the rest of your life. Consider these points before you decide what beer to have on the third-biggest day in a Man's life.

How Many?

How many people are going to be drinking? Figure every adult will drink at least three beers. When you factor in those babies that don't with those that do, and subtract for how much the kids are stealing, it should average out. Depending on the number of people, you may want to consider getting one or more kegs.

What Will It Cost?

Are you going for premium or imported stuff? Or are your guests not going to notice the difference in the beer once the piñata is bashed open?

How Drunk Will They Get?

This is something to consider: It's one thing if they get really "crazy" with the suds and Uncle Frank heads out to the dance floor without his shoes. It's quite another if the best man and his old lady are riding his hog doing doughnuts on the lawn.

Who's Paying?

This is the clincher: Traditionally the bride's father picked up the check for all things wedding, but then again, she was *traditionally* a virgin. However, if the old geezer is dumb

enough or loaded enough to cover the cost, go with top-shelf brew and lots of it. As the father of the bride, he really shouldn't make too much of a stink about cost, considering you're going to be taking his little angel off his hands for the next six years or so.

Tradition

According to extensive research—in other words, the first thing Google spat up—beer has a rich history in the wedding tradition. When a man got hitched in ancient Babylon, it was apparently the practice that the father of the bride provided his new son-in-law with not only his hot Babylonian daughter, but also all the mead he could drink for a month. In case you haven't been to the Xena convention in a while, mead is a honey-derived beer, and the Babylonian calendar was lunar based.

Yeah, so? Well, this twenty-eight-day period of free brew was allegedly called the "honey month." Giving us what we know today as the "honeymoon." Which goes to show that marriages are like parties: great at first, but once the beer runs out, it's all downhill.

LUBE JOB

For thousands of years,

beer has been a great social lubricant. It's been the ice-breaker for a billion conversations. Sure, the great majority of them have been pointless, self-serving diatribes that we regret ever getting involved in. No doubt there is some level of Hell where damned souls spend eternity, forced to listen to their half of every drunken conversation they've ever had. But every Man has had a couple of booze-fueled talks that have garnered him lifelong friends and gotten him laid.

That's the magic of beer. It's a bonding agent that's sitting in a keg, at the nearest bar, just waiting for you to go out and make friends . . . or at least drop your pants in public.

THE "AFTER WORK" BEER

The tradition of the after work beer is dying off. In this post-digital era, people are too busy. We're running around, paying bills, picking up the kids, checking e-mails, evading the police. Who has time for the after work beer anymore?

The after work beer probably goes all the way back to some primitive after-the-hunt ritual. It was a time for prehistoric males to bullshit with each other, prehistoric style. Just as contemporary men do when they share an after work beer, cave men would probably talk about stuff from their day, like "Thanks for the help, that bush pig was moving fast," or "Cool spear, where'd you get it?" and "Hey, I think we're going to have a really strong third quarter with the Anderson account."

Maybe all they had to drink back then was water, or some animal blood, but it didn't matter because it was still a *bonding ritual* shared over a *drink.* And you should do your part to make sure this three-hundred-thousand-year-old tradition lives on with an after work beer and a coworker you don't despise.

The after work beer can have a definite downside. Your buddy from work might have a big mouth. Now *everyone's* gonna know you think the people in Accounting are dickheads. That female coworker is going to look pretty good after five or six beers and you just might find yourself getting into a workplace romance. Remember, in nine out of ten cases, people are fired for getting blow jobs in the supply room.

So don't overdo it. You have to work tomorrow and before that you've got to drive home tonight. For that reason, let's review the legal blood alcohol content for the fifty states, the District of Columbia, and Puerto Rico, where Medalla beer and Puerto Ricans come from.

DRINKING AND DRIVING STATE BY STATE

State	BAC defined as illegal per se[1]	Administrative license suspension 1st offense?[2]	Restore driving privileges during suspension?[2,3]	Do penalties include interlock/ forfeiture?[4]
ALABAMA	0.08	90 days	no	no/no
ALASKA	0.08	90 days	after 30 days	yes/yes
ARIZONA	0.08	90 days	after 30 days	yes/yes
ARKANSAS	0.08	120 days	yes	yes/yes
CALIFORNIA	0.08	4 months	after 30 days	yes/yes
COLORADO	0.10	3 months	yes	yes/no
CONNECTICUT	0.08	90 days	yes	no/no
DELAWARE	0.10	3 months	no	yes/no
DISTRICT OF COLUMBIA	0.08	2–90 days	yes	no/no
FLORIDA	0.08	6 months	yes	yes/no
GEORGIA	0.08	1 year	yes	yes/yes
HAWAII	0.08	3 months	after 30 days	yes/no
IDAHO	0.08	90 days	after 30 days	yes/no
ILLINOIS	0.08	3 months	after 30 days	yes/yes
INDIANA	0.08	180 days	after 30 days	yes/no
IOWA	0.10	180 days	yes	yes/no
KANSAS	0.08	30 days	no	yes/no
KENTUCKY	0.08	—	—	yes/yes
LOUISIANA	0.08	90 days	after 30 days	yes/yes
MAINE	0.08	90 days	yes	yes/yes
MARYLAND	0.08	45 days	yes	yes/no
MASSACHUSETTS	0.08[1]	90 days	no	no/no
MICHIGAN	0.10	—	—	yes/yes
MINNESOTA	0.10	90 days	after 15 days	no/yes
MISSISSIPPI	0.08	90 days	no	yes/yes
MISSOURI	0.08	30 days	no	yes/yes
MONTANA	0.10	—	—	yes/yes
NEBRASKA	0.08	90 days	after 30 days	yes/no
NEVADA	0.10	90 days	after 45 days	yes/no
NEW HAMPSHIRE	0.08	6 months	no	yes/no
NEW JERSEY	0.10	—	—	yes/no
NEW MEXICO	0.08	90 days	after 30 days	yes/no
NEW YORK	0.08	variable[5]	yes	yes/yes
NORTH CAROLINA	0.08	30 days	after 10 days	yes/yes

State	BAC defined as illegal per se[1]	Administrative license suspension 1st offense?[2]	Restore driving privileges during suspension?[2,3]	Do penalties include interlock/ forfeiture?[4]
NORTH DAKOTA	0.10	91 days	after 30 days	yes/yes
OHIO	0.10	90 days	after 15 days	yes/yes
OKLAHOMA	0.08	180 days	yes	yes/yes
OREGON	0.08	90 days	after 30 days	yes/yes
PENNSYLVANIA	0.10	—	—	yes/yes
RHODE ISLAND	0.08	—	—	yes/yes
SOUTH CAROLINA	0.10	—	—	yes/yes
SOUTH DAKOTA	0.08	—	—	no/no
TENNESSEE	0.08	—	—	yes/yes
TEXAS	0.08	90 days	yes	yes/yes
UTAH	0.08	90 days	no	yes/no
VERMONT	0.08	90 days	no	no/yes
VIRGINIA	0.08	7 days	no	yes/no
WASHINGTON	0.08	90 days	after 30 days	yes/yes
WEST VIRGINIA	0.10	6 months	after 30 days	yes/no
WISCONSIN	0.10	6 months	yes	yes/yes
WYOMING	0.08	90 days	yes	no/no
PUERTO RICO	0.08	—	—	—

1 The law in Massachusetts is not a per se law. A BAC of 0.08 percent in Massachusetts is evidence of alcohol impairment but isn't illegal per se.

2 Information pertains to drivers in violation of the BAC defined as illegal per se for all drivers, not the special BAC for young drivers.

3 Drivers usually must demonstrate special hardship to justify restoring privileges during suspension, and then privileges often are restricted.

4 A multiple offender's vehicle may be seized and disposed.

5 In New York, administrative license suspension lasts until prosecution is complete.

The above chart is provided by OHS, Inc., to you through the courtesy of the Insurance Institute for Highway Safety, Highway Loss Data Institute, http://www.highwaysafety.org. Last modified: 10-Jan-2003.
Source: http://www.ohsinc.com/drunk_driving_laws_blood_breath%20_alcohol_limits_CHART.htm

TOASTS: WHAT TO SAY WHEN YOU DON'T HAVE ANY DEAD HOMIES

Unless you're doing it because your woman's gone and done you wrong, drinking is typically a social activity. And therein lies the problem: Social activities usually require "talking"—not a strong suit for a lot of men. That's why you need to learn a great toast. A great toast usually rhymes, and the best ones are always dirty. The next time you're out pounding beers, pop the top on one of these classics.

Here's to our wives and girlfriends . . .
may they never meet.

Here's to Eve, the Mother of our race,
She wore her fig leaf in the proper place.
Here's to Adam, who got to know her
And soon invented the first leaf blower.

Here's to women, whose greatest skill I can tell
Is getting milk from a nut without cracking the shell.

Here's to the wound that never heals,
The more you poke it, the better it feels!

To all my friends, may there only come honors . . .
on her tits, on her ass, on her face, and on her often.

Here's to a long life and a merry one,
A quick death and an easy one,
A pretty girl and an honest one,
A cold beer, and another one!

With one of these gems, everyone will be impressed with your wit and you can get back to drinking . . . and brooding about that dang woman what done you wrong.

BEER: THE GATEKEEPER
TO MALE EMOTION

Men aren't raised to be very open about their feelings. By the age of ten, most boys learn that expressing vulnerability will get them mocked and beaten. Only when four or five more years have passed, and they begin drinking large quantities of beer, can these same guys open up and express any emotion other than *anger,* as in when a favorite team loses, or *sadness,* as in when a favorite team loses.

Beer gives such men a way to say things they'd otherwise never be able to say. It may take some men thirteen beers before they can say "I love you" to another friend, their fathers, or their fourteenth beer. The most common examples of beer-induced affection are "I fuckin' love you, man," and "I *can't* punch you in the face, because I fuckin' love you, man."

The fact that men, and some teenagers, can't say such things until they've dusted off a case of cheap beer between them is not to say the sentiment isn't real. Especially when it's been backed up with some sort of blood ritual. In the contemporary era, the blood ritual between men has evolved to fit the times. It could be as simple as poking their fingers with a pin and letting their blood intermingle, or as intricate as jointly murdering the girl one of them loved, but never had the guts to talk to.

Yes, men expressing love with the aid of beer is a good thing. The only problem is how to make them stop. Word to the wise: After the twenty-sixth "I love you, man," it loses some of its cathartic appeal and is only going to get you mocked or beaten.

FIRST BEER WITH DAD

T here are few events in father-and-son bonding that are as momentous as when Dad first offers his son a beer. Like a frosty torch handed from one generation to the next, this gesture marks the moment that before your father passed into the *next* world, he looked you in the eye as a Man, and shared one of life's greatest gifts in *this* one.

Every beer drinker has his own story; mine takes place back in the late 1970s. That first beer with my dad was a rite of passage, an unforgettable milestone that ranks up there with my first slow dance, my first kiss, my first time firing a gun, and my first time getting arrested—what a night.

My father had gotten caught up in the CB radio craze and bought himself a giant antenna that had to be installed on the roof of our house in Chicago. An easy job for him, but he knew he'd need a helper small enough to make his way through the narrow crawlspaces of our attic. At twelve years old, I was selected from his seven children. I would fasten nuts onto the bolts my dad would have to drill through our roof, to keep the twenty-five-foot antenna from falling into nearby power lines, burning down our house, and killing us all.

Of course, you don't want to do a job with this much difficulty and danger in the daytime. No, the old man figured he could stagger around on the steep roof of our house after a long day at work, in the dark, in the middle of winter.

Nevertheless, late that night, after we'd spent a couple hours of yelling to each other through the roof of our house, the job was done. Afterward, we sat down, two weary, dirty workers in the kitchen. With his familiar request, "Get your poor father a beer," I was back to my old job of going to the icy back porch to fetch him a can of Old Style from one of the many cases he kept as his private reserve. Then, as I rose from my chair, it happened. He said those unforgettable words, "And get one for yourself."

Instantly I knew my life had changed. My dad had just told me to drink with him. Like an out-of-body experience, I was thrown into a surreal state. Time seemed to stop from the anticipation of the great event about to happen. It's a strange, conscious dis-orientation akin to that which I would one day feel in the moments before the first time I got laid.

I returned with two beers and sat in the kitchen, as if in a dream, quietly sipping a nearly frozen beer with my hero, my role model, my dad. After a while he broke the silence. "You know, we don't really talk enough." Not believing this was actually happening, I still couldn't speak. "Uh-huh."

He continued, "You're getting older now and I've wanted to have this talk to you for a while . . . about your role in this house." There I was, on the brink of manhood with the only giant I'd ever known about to welcome me into that exclusive world. I listened, as one about to knighted, for my dad to say the words that told me he knew I was now a Man. He looked me in the eye, furrowing his brow, and then he spoke. "Have you been stealing my beer off the back porch?"

THE BEER PROMISE

Hey, let's get together sometime for a beer." You've said it so many times, but that time never seems to come. Then, weeks or months later, you run into that guy again. And once more the words are exchanged. "Let's grab a beer sometime." "Yeah, that sounds good, man." Surely he knows that the likelihood of you two ever getting together for that beer is slim to none.

He's someone you went to school with, or a coworker from your last job. He's a guy you met at a friend's party who seemed okay. A neighbor who helped you move. A former teammate. A guy who was in your band. An old army buddy. Life is full of guys for whom you'd like to make time to have a beer. But you seldom do.

Just like you, men all over are doing the same thing. Why do we say those words, only to blow off the follow-up? Do we really mean them? Certainly "Let's get a beer sometime" has more intent than "See ya later." It's an invitation to meet again to bond, laugh, and reminisce as men have for thousands of years over a sacred brew.

And what of all that beer that goes unconsumed? It sits lonely, as if on the Island of Misfit Toys, facing its expiration date, waiting for you to hold true to your promise. That beer is going to go bad. The purpose for which it was put on this earth will be forever unfulfilled. In a perfect world, there'd be nothing but time to get together over all those promised beers.

Next time you're sitting at home watching the game by yourself, pick up the phone, call one of those guys, and tell him to meet you down at the bar. Take turns buying each other one frosty, delicious tall glass of beer after another. Savor its hoppy aroma. Enjoy the beer's ice-cold wetness as it fills your mouth. Maybe even split a plate of chicken wings. And the next time you say, "Let's get together again and have a beer," mean it.

A message from the American Council of Poultry Parts Distributors

THE DESIGNATED DRIVER

"**D**rink Responsibly." We've all heard it. But it's not just another slogan a certain giant brewing company uses to downplay their part in our highway death toll. Truth is, because of a few tens of thousands of people every year who can't handle their suds, you and I now have to worry about the highway patrol's cherries popping up in our rearview.

Gone are the days when you could merrily speed down the darkened street, tossing empties at the parked cars you've just sideswiped. Now, if you're going out to pound a few with a buddy, one of you must drink responsibly in order to drive you both home. But how do you know if you're too drunk to drive? There are signs:

For example, if at some point during your night of beer guzzling, you find yourself pissing into an empty beer bottle—for *ANY* reason—you've most likely had too much to drink and shouldn't drive.

However, if you see your buddy mistakenly drink from that same bottle, and notice that he doesn't recoil from the flavor of your hearty ammonia beverage—be responsible and grab his keys. He's drunker than you are. You're driving tonight.

SIDE NOTE: *If you watch your friend chug a beer that you just "warm filtered" an hour before and you get a* boner, *you should switch to Kristal, because you're gay.*

Also, as our lawyers have asked me to point out, a dead **MAN SHOW** *viewer is of no use to anyone. Please consult the chart for blood alcohol content at the beginning of this chapter so you don't end up as sticky pink goo in a twisted pile of burnt metal, rubber, and glass.*

AT THE PARTY

Was the last party

you went to a total drag? Are you a social pariah because your last party was a dull, boring affair with everyone going home early? Whether you're a party thrower or goer, you're sure to benefit from this section. If you take a little time to glean what you can from these pages, you'll make friends at the next party without having to swallow anything weird or show your scar.

TEN PARTY SURVIVAL TIPS

1. When you attend a big party, it's always a nice gesture to bring beer. But be sure to bring crappy beer and then upgrade by drinking the good stuff someone else brought.

2. Drink the bottled beer from the fridge first, before moving on to the keg. It's usually better beer and you won't have to stand around waiting. Eventually you'll be drunk enough that the taste of the crap in the keg will go unnoticed.

3. The best way to find the lost bottle opener is to finish off, or hide, the *canned* beer. Suddenly everyone's looking for the bottle opener, and you can believe *someone* will find it.

4. Until a keg is almost empty, it won't need more than two or three pumps to keep pressure. Pump it any more than that and you'll get foam.

5. Don't eat anything that's been out for more than twenty minutes. That's about how long it takes for at least one guy with piss on his hands to paw his way through the tray.

6. Forget about ever using the bathroom. It's most likely crowded with girls doing their makeup, talking, or passing out. As soon as they vacate, the can is taken over by people doing drugs they don't want to share with you. You're going to have to whiz wherever you can. Be creative. Let a window, someone else's bottle, or a sock drawer inspire you. Never set your own bottle down.

7. Sometimes the beer runs out at a party and it's too late to go to the store. Lucky for you every girl at the party has left at least three half-finished beers in her wake. Just tell yourself that their backwash is made from the very same spit you've wanted to swap with them all night. By now you're loaded and you won't taste the urine anyway.

8. When it gets late, always keep a watchful eye as you're talking to a girl who's drinking beer from a cup. One of you is going to end up wearing it.

9. Always bring a buddy to pawn off on her cock-blocking friend.

10. Don't hang around too late. If you're one of the last guys there, you're gonna look like a jerk when you don't make an effort to help clean up at least a little bit. Who needs to feel guilt? You're already teeming with remorse over the CDs you've stuffed in your coat.

KEGSTANDS

The object of doing a kegstand is to drink as much as you can, for as long as you can, without stopping. It's kind of like what's already going on at the rest of the party, only you'll be upside down. Unless you want to find out how that girl in your Psych class ended up with a neck brace, here's the checklist for a successful kegstand: a keg, two assistants, and a mouth. Leaving out any one of these three could lead to disaster.

Take a hold on the keg with both hands. Have your friends grab you by your feet and tip you upward until you're upside down, doing a handstand on the keg. Have your friend put the tap in your mouth and fire away. What a country we live in. You're drinking beer like a fish—upside down!

Be sure to have a predetermined signal that you're done drinking. For most, the "cough beer through your nose and gasp for air while they spray you in the face" seems to work.

THE BEER BONG

It's just a simple device made of a funnel and a plastic tube. Beer is poured into the funnel, it exits through a tube and enters the mouth. Its exact origin is unknown but it most likely involves some hick in a garage, gasoline, and blindness. Still, countless men owe a great debt to the beer bong, especially when it's used by a *woman*.

With each round she spends sucking on the business end of a beer bong, the girl who tries to keep up with the guys is saying, "Somebody please shoot irresponsibility down my windpipe! I can't wait to have impaired judgment!" It's her mating call, her copulation clarion with the beer bong as her trumpet. For this reason, to many guys, the beer bong has been the deciding factor in getting laid at a party. It's the great equalizer that gives everyone an even shot at the girl who's willing to lower her standards as she clings to her last strains of consciousness.

The beer bong's greatest attribute is the speed at which it delivers poor judgment. The brew is inside her so fast that half your work is done. That hour or more usually spent waiting for her to down four or five drinks is miraculously compressed into a few brief minutes. It's the closest Man has come to time travel. In fact, if you can get her to drink vodka through the beer bong, you'll be transported to an incredible future . . . providing she doesn't barf on your cock in the car.

YARD OF BEER

T he yard of beer is drunk from a tall, narrow glass about—you guessed it—three feet long. At its base the glass is fat and bulbous. At the top of its long neck it flares out like a trumpet. The yard of beer is the primitive version of the beer bong invented in the days before PVC tubing and date rape. It holds about 48 ounces of beer and usually come with a wooden stand to rest it on between sips. But only a girl would *sip* out of one of these things. You gotta just pick it up and go for it.

By the time you've finished off the beer in the bell, you're holding the thing out at about 80 degrees. Now you can see down into the neck of the glass. The beer keeps coming, but you're okay, you're in the groove. And suddenly—*glorp!* The bulb at the bottom is flushing the beer down your throat almost faster than you can drink it. Almost. By the way, unless you're gulping a manly stout or porter from one of these things, you're a pussy. No yellowy piss beer allowed!

You can buy them in specialty stores, but if they don't have them and you've got balls, you can usually swipe one from almost any bar with the words "Ye Olde . . ." in its name. And don't let the yard of beer's whole "Renaissance Faire" vibe throw you. A couple of these will put you right where you want to be—well above the legal limit.

EDWARD 40 HANDS

Every now and then a movie comes along that makes a profound change in the nation's culture. *Jaws* made people afraid of the water. *Saturday Night Fever* made people want to dance. *Flashdance* made girls all over the country want to get out there and weld.

Such is the case with Tim Burton's *Edward Scissorhands.* This film about a misunderstood outcast with scissors for hands touched the nation's heart. Today, in frat houses, in college dorms, and at barbecues, people pay homage to that movie, but in a different way.

Here's a great way to spice up your next party. Get a roll of duct tape. Now take two 40-ounce bottles of your favorite malt liquor. Have your friends tape a "40" to each of your hands.

You are now like Edward, a prisoner of your deformity. All that stands between you and the normal people is a mere 80 ounces of pretty amber rocket fuel with an 8% alcohol content. The deal is you can't take them off your hands until they are both empty. Nighty-night. Oh, by the way, someone is going to have to help you pee.

KEGS TO RICHE$!™

E veryone knows keg parties are a great way to get out, meet people, and get hammered. But did you know they're also ripe with fantastic business opportunities? It's true. And the best thing about this Kegs to Riche$™ plan is that it doesn't require all that creepy schmoozing and glad-handing that most financial ventures entail. In fact, it works even better when you remain anonymous, and it's as simple as 1-2-3!

Step One: The Setup

This is the easiest step because you've already done this many times. Simply enjoy yourself at the party. Dance, eat, drink. Be merry even, because you're just two more steps away from the riches that come from being a player in the world of finance!

Step Two: The Pitch

This step is the most important on your way to untold profits. Like all great financial opportunities, this one requires just the right timing. Your fantastic pitch should come only after you've had your fill of beer and song and you're on the way to the door to go home. This is the supreme moment to pitch your incredible proposition to your prospective business partners! Why? Because when everyone sees you're about to head out the door, they immediately realize they're at a crossroads: It's do or die time to get in on the ground floor of your incredible offer. And what is your offer? You're now looking for investors. Investors in the new keg, which you're just leaving to buy!

Step Three: The Close

You've propositioned your new partners, now it's time to close the deal and gather that start-up money, say five or six bucks from each. But remember: Too many associates on your board of directors can expose your new enterprise to the volatility of the market.

We're working from a much leaner business model here. Three to four people, max. Now, simply take that crisp, green venture capital out the door and go get a slice of pizza to soak up all that free beer you just drank. After you actualize your expenses—food, bus fare, and a skin mag—you'll be happy to see that after only one night in business you've already cleared ten to twenty dollars of pure profit. Congratulations! You are now well on your way to financial freedom!

Another great way to earn profits at the party is, right after you leave, stand outside the door and charge the next arriving group of people three bucks a head to get in. You're on your way to being a party tycoon!

Warning:

It's long been known that certain people make better business partners than others. The owner of the house and any of his close associates are *bad* choices. Stick with the solitary, skinny guys who look like they don't belong at the keg party in the first place. At this stage of your financial empire, you're better off with low-risk, silent partners whose ass you can kick should they attempt a hostile takeover.

WHO GETS THE LAST BEER?

At many parties there comes a time when you find there's only one beer left. How do you decide who should get to drink it? Is there a beer etiquette? Here is a list of criteria that should be considered when deciding who is entitled to the privilege of the Last Beer.

Who's still awake?

Who paid for it?

Who hasn't had a beer in a while?

Who is one beer away from hooking up?

Who is not drunk enough?

Who is the smartest?

Who most needs it?

Who is shipping off to Nam?

Who had the final beer last time?

Who has a hook for a hand?

Who recently got dumped?

Who hasn't puked . . . in the last hour?

Who once murdered a drifter?

If you have answered "me" to any one of these questions, grab that beer and gulp it down before anyone else notices what's going on.

MAN-O-VATION:
LAST BEER SAVER

Never again will you go to your fridge and find someone else has already snagged your last beer. Using the latest in cutting-edge beer protection technology, the Lectro-Brew 9000 is guaranteed to save the last one for you.

The Lectro-Brew 9000's electrodes clamp to any bottle cap or can, completing a circuit that delivers three successive jolts of current rated at 480 volts at 30 amps at time of closure, gently warning your beer-truder that the Last Beer always goes to the host.

When it's time for your Last Beer, simply pull the circuit breaker, unclench your guest's locked fingers from your bottle and pop the top. It's just that easy!

Also available: an adaptor for Corona, Dos Equis, and Tecate that sends three 9mm rounds, with a muzzle velocity of 760 feet per second, into your guest's torso, kindly informing him, *"no mas."*

GETTING THE BEER SMELL
OUT OF YOUR CARPET

Getting the stale beer stank out of your carpet isn't as hard as you might think. There are a couple of different approaches.

THE WRONG WAY: Rent a rug cleaner/shampooer. You'll end up dropping about twenty-five to thirty bucks and missing most of the game while you try to wrestle an awkward, messy unit around your place.

THE RIGHT WAY: As the sun comes up, or before going to bed, whichever comes first, sprinkle a light, even dusting of baking soda over the entire carpet. Go ahead and dump extra wherever there was a spill. When you come to, six to nineteen hours later, bust out the vacuum and clean it up. It won't even take too long, leaving you plenty of time to get back into the ol' fart sack should the howl of the vacuum make you long for the peace of your darkened bedroom.

The best part is, a whole box of baking soda will cost you about a dollar. You just saved twenty-five bucks and a backache. But remember, this method only works on odors, not stains (e.g., *vomit*). You may want to buy a fresh box *before* the party. The thing about baking soda is, once it's absorbed enough odors, it develops the power to leave them behind. If you use the box that's been in your fridge for the last year, you'll end up with a carpet that smells like a combination of beer, onions, and ass. This is a scent that's commonly known as the "Ghost of George Wendt."

KICK IT UP A NOTCH:
BEER DRINKS

Ever since the first time

someone in the Wild West got their ass dragged along the length of a bar, and some other desperate slob licked up the spill, people have realized beer tastes great when mixed with other booze. From that day forward creative types and people who need to get whacked out of their skulls in a hurry have been mixing beer drinks. Here are the only ones you really need to know. They're basic and don't require anything too exotic or queer.

BOILERMAKER

This is the granddaddy of them all. Its origins go back to the simple "shot and a beer" order that two-fisted drinkers have been calling for whenever they needed to put the hammer down. This drink was probably "invented" by an amputee as a way to keep up with the guys who *didn't* get an arm torn off in the boiler room . . . or the sheet metal press, or in a combine or wood chipper or . . . Well, you get the idea.

INGREDIENTS
2 oz. whiskey
10 oz. beer

GLASS TYPE
Shot glass
Mug

DIRECTIONS
Fill shot glass with whiskey.
Drop full shot glass into a mug full of beer.
Drink immediately and repeatedly.
Say g'night.

Alcohol (ABV) 10% (21 proof)

CAR BOMB

God bless the Irish. You won't find many froufrou drinks in an Irish bar. It just wouldn't seem right to have fruity drinks in any place that still has piss from before the Easter Rising on the bathroom floor.

But check out the simple refinement they gave to what would otherwise be a standard boilermaker. Here the aptly named "Car Bomb" adds just a bit of sweetness to the mix for the lady alcoholic. Try using John Power & Son Irish whiskey, a favorite at the *Man Show.*

INGREDIENTS
1/2 shot Irish whiskey
1/2 shot Baileys Irish Cream
1 pint Guinness stout

GLASS TYPE
Shot glass
Pint glass

DIRECTIONS
Using proportions of 50/50, combine Baileys Irish Cream and Irish whiskey into one shot glass. Drop the shot into a mug of Guinness and chug until empty. Repeat five or six times and then challenge someone to a fight.

Alcohol (ABV) 5% (11 proof)

SNAKE BITE

A nother drink that takes two simple things and mixes them together! This time, it's beer and cider. A night of staggering and urinating in public couldn't be easier.

INGREDIENTS

1/2 pint lager
1/2 pint dry or sweet cider

GLASS TYPE

Beer mug

DIRECTIONS

Pour ingredients into a pint glass.
Drink.
Hit on a few chicks.
Give up.
Repeat steps 1-2 as necessary. Fall over.

Alcohol (ABV) 5% (10 proof)

RED FLOW

Sometimes known as a "Juggy's Monthly Visit," this classic mix of tomato juice and beer can be a fine drink for its own sake, or just the thing when you need a little "hair of the dog." Adjust the amount of tomato juice to fit your particular hangover.

INGREDIENTS
Cold beer
Tomato juice

GLASS TYPE
Beer mug

DIRECTIONS
Fill a beer mug with beer, top off with a shot or two of tomato juice. Pull down the shades and go back to bed.

BLACK AND TAN

This is another beer beverage whose name goes back to the troubled history of Ireland. The Black and Tans were specially recruited auxiliary troops the Brits sent to Ireland to help the Royal Irish Constabulary take on the IRA in Northern Ireland.

With their khaki uniforms, black hats and belts, they were purportedly given the name Black and Tans after a well-known pack of hounds in Limerick. It's yet to be determined which Black and Tans have caused Irish Republicans more headaches, the troops or the drink. Remeber those Republican patriots when you're on your knees in the can, and the guy in the stall next to you is dropping off that free buffet he converted into a "stink pickle."

INGREDIENTS
1 part Bass pale ale
1 part Guinness stout

GLASS TYPE
Mug or pint glass

DIRECTIONS
Fill your mug half full with Bass ale.
Next, pour Guinness over a spoon slowly until glass is full. If done correctly, the Guinness will stay on top and the Bass on bottom, hence the name Black and Tan. Repeat 5 or 6 times. Try to hold back a tear during "Four Green Fields."

GEORGE WASHINGTON'S BEER RECIPE

Given that the greatest beer drink is beer itself, here is a recipe that was used by your first president and mine, George Washington. Ol' timber teeth liked his beer and kept an ample supply at Mount Vernon. This recipe comes from his manuscript collections preserved in the New York Public Library. How did New York get its dirty hands on something that probably belongs in George's home back in Ol' Virginny? The same way the Yankees get a pennant: They buy them. Here's what George had to say on the matter:

TO MAKE SMALL BEER

Take a large Siffer [Sifter] full of Bran Hops to your Taste—Boil these 3 hours then strain out 30 Gall[ons] into a cooler put in 3 Gall[ons] Molasses while the Beer is Scalding hot or rather draw the Molasses into the cooler & St[r]ain the Beer on it while boiling Hot. let this stand till it is little more than Blood warm then put in a quart of Yea[s]t if the Weather is very Cold cover it over with a Blank[et] & let it Work in the Cooler 24 hours then put it into the Cask—leave the bung open till it is almost don[e] Working—Bottle it that day Week it was Brewed. Cool and consume.

The first thing is obvious. The spelling in this recipe would make George Bush enroll George Washington in a No Child Left Behind program. Perhaps he was drunk on his own stuff. You'd have to be to leave your bung hole open that long.

The second thing we learn is that this simple recipe gives you an ass-kicking brew with twice the alcohol of modern mass-produced suds. At nearly 11% by volume, six or seven of these could make Martha look hotter than any one of George's slaves. So here's what you do next time you're back east and you see one of these landmark signs.

GEORGE WASHINGTON SLEPT HERE

LET THE GAMES BEGIN

It's true they seem

to be played mostly by younger drinkers, but no book on beer would be complete without a section on drinking games. These next games were chosen by virtue of their simplicity and their fun quotient. Though there's no real unit of measure for fun, all of these will make you want to get together with friends and play, regardless of your age. Just remember, if you really want to be a competitor, you have to *train*.

A NOTE TO YOUNG DRINKERS: Do not be frightened by all the text you're about to see. Sure, it looks intimidating—having to read nearly a *whole* page just to get shit-faced. That's probably more than you read all semester. But don't worry, the writing is supposed to be *entertaining*.

By the way, you must be twenty-one years of age blah blah blah. . . . More importantly, if you play one of these games and die of alcohol poisoning, puke on your girlfriend, crash your car, or try to fly off a building, you're officially an idiot and can't sue us.

TWENTY-ONE

You'll need: cups, beer, table, and chairs.

This is a memory game for three or more players at a table. Decide whether play will start from the left or the right. Once the direction of play is decided, the first player says the number "one." The next player follows, saying the number "two." Play goes around the table, with each player saying a number, in order until they reach 21. If anyone says a wrong number before reaching 21, they must drink from their cup of beer. (Yeah, it seems unlikely, but have you spoken to a college student lately?) Congratulations, whoever reaches 21, you've just made it to drinking age. Suck it up 'cause you have to drink.

After finishing the required drink, the person who has just said "twenty-one" gets to make up a new rule for the number sequence. Could be anything. Be creative.

EXAMPLES:

Switch number 2 for number 9.

Instead of saying number 15, you tap on the table three times.

On any prime number you must say "cock."

Skip all multiples of 5.

On 17, you kiss the member of the opposite sex nearest you.

On the number 13, you spit in your neighbor's beer.

Play resumes in the opposite direction, with the new rule in effect for the rest of the game. When 21 is reached again, that person must drink and another new rule gets added. It gets tricky because players have to remember *all* of the rules as they go along.

The main rules to remember are: You say a wrong number, you must drink and play resumes in the opposite direction. A new rule is added *only* when 21 is reached.

VEGETABLES

If you're into group drinking games, this is a great one because it has very few requirements. It can be played sitting at a table, or on the floor. There's no soiled quarter to dig out of your glass, and there are no dice being banged on a table. All you need is plenty of beer and people with nothing better to do.

Everyone sits in a circle. Each person then selects a vegetable before the game begins. The first person to finish chugging his beer gets to go first. Play begins with that person saying the name of their own vegetable, followed by the name of someone else's vegetable. That second person called must now say their own vegetable and then say someone else's. You can't go back to the person who called you. Sounds kind of dumb, right? "What's the point," you're saying. "Boo-hoo. I want to go back a page and play Twenty-one again."

Well, here's the catch: At no time during the game can any of your teeth be visible. If someone sees any part of your teeth while you're saying a vegetable, you have to drink. Even if it's not your turn to say a vegetable, and someone sees your teeth, you have to drink.

So there you are trying to say "baby carrots" with your lips covering your teeth like you've lost your dentures. And you look like a retard. Which will make other people laugh—and have to drink. Get it? You possess the power to make others laugh, show their teeth, and have to drink.

Now you can raise your game by saying the vegetables in funny ways. Cross your eyes, grab your wang, and say "lima beans" in someone's face. They laughing? Good, 'cause now they're drinking. Okay, now let go of your dick; it's the other person's turn. Remember, if anyone sees *your* teeth, you have to drink.

MEDICATION TIME

This isn't so much a game as it is a speed course to getting toasted. There are no tricky rules. Nothing to memorize. No special skills. If you can tip a glass, you can play.

TOOLS REQUIRED:
   One analog clock with a second hand
   Lots of your favorite beer

Each person chooses a number from one to twelve. If there are more than twelve players, people can share a number. Players fill their cups or grab ahold of their cans/bottles of beer. The clock is set in motion. As the second hand sweeps by your number, it's medication time. Take a big drink. That's all there is to it. Each time your number comes up, you take a huge gulp.

This game has a beautifully poetic fatalism to it. At first it seems to take forever for your turn to come around. But after a while, the time seems to go faster. And then, faster still. There's no escape from the second hand. It just keeps coming around and around. Each time you drink. And you drink some more. And you keep drinking. And you drink even more. More and more beer with each passing minute. Is it a dream come true, or is it a nightmare?

MORE BEER. MORE BEER! MORE BEER!! WILL IT EVER END?!

Yes. Yes, it does.

The game ends when the beer is gone, nobody is left conscious, or the clock can't be read because it's covered with puke. This game is best played with dudes, since really, the point of it is to pass out drunk. Heeeey, wait a second . . .

BEER BASEBALL

This game is a combination of our fabled National Pastime, baseball, and the country's real national pastime, getting sloshed.

GEAR:

Softball gear
A field
Plastic cups
Lots of beer

A cup of beer is placed at each base. The game is played exactly as you would play regular softball *except* that each time a runner reaches a base, he or she has to chug the cup of beer waiting there. The runner cannot advance to the next base until the cup is empty.

For example, let's say a batter hits one deep into the outfield. Normally, this could be a double or triple, but that all depends on how fast the runner can slurp down the beer at each base. You'll find that as the guy who belted a homer crosses the plate, he isn't quite the same boy he was when he first picked up the bat.

Only the batter drinks as he goes around the bases. Once a runner is on base, he doesn't drink again until he scores a run. The team that's at bat is responsible for keeping the cups full of beer. If they blow it and forget to fill the cup, the runner has to wait for the cup to be filled before he can advance to the next base, even if the ball is still rolling around in the outfield.

Adding beer to the mix raises the stakes on the usual company softball game. Try committing intentional errors in the field when your boss is at the plate. "Oh, my God, *another* inside-the-park home run! Way to go, big guy. Drink up." And how is it that every time the boss is at bat, the cups are bigger? Hmmm . . . By the third inning he's so stewed, he's promising everyone a raise.

POT LUCK

Although any number can partake, this game is best played at a bar with four to six friends and a pitcher of beer. It can be played at home, but if you don't have a pitcher, you can use a pot. Hence the name.

Each player kicks in a couple bucks for the first pitcher. Next a player starts drinking straight from the pitcher. This person can drink as little or as much as he or she wants. When done, he passes the pitcher to the next player. This player follows suit, drinking as much as desired and passing the pitcher on.

Eventually, someone is going to finish off that pitcher. Either by drinking half or more, or by having only the last mouthful, the pitcher will be emptied. The person who finishes off the pitcher is declared the "winner."

More importantly, the person who drank *immediately before* the winner is the loser. As the loser, he or she has to buy the next pitcher. As you can see, it's more important not to be the loser than it is to be the winner.

A big pitcher helps because it's harder to judge just how much beer you should drink. One thing that makes this game fun is that alliances will form as people work together to make a specific person buy the next pitcher—again and again and again.

This game gets the *Man Show* Drinking Game Seal of Approval because it's guaranteed to get you stone drunk, or get you a brand-new cold sore.

DONKEY KONG

C ◀ **AUTION:** *The following game should be played* only *when you've decided you no longer want to reside in your apartment, rented home, or dorm.*

To play Donkey Kong, you'll need some preparation, namely extensive drinking. Not the "Wow, that was some party" kind of drinking. I mean the "What time did the cops shut us down? We killed four kegs and all my fish" kind of drinking. This is the kind of game you may only get to play once in your life, but if you're jackass stupid, you'll have a good time.

Just like the classic video game it's named after, this game tests your ability to dodge empty kegs. You stand at the bottom of a flight of stairs; your idiot buddy stands at the top with the empty kegs. As he rolls the kegs down the stairs, you try to climb up, jumping the kegs as they approach. The only rule is you cannot touch the kegs. Take turns. Laugh. Make the best of your hangover, and then find a new place to live.

SPORTS

Why is it guys

who really love beer also have a deep love for sports? Why is it guys who really love sports also end up becoming low-life gamblers who also drink beer? It's because sports and beer bring out similar qualities in men: bonding, brother-hood, and brawling. If you've ever had the misfortune of wearing the wrong cap in the Shea Stadium bleachers, this fact was no doubt made all too clear to you. Despite your lumps, this chapter will help Men appreciate the volatile combination that beer mixed with sports is meant to be.

RECREATIONAL BEER SPORTS

Beer and recreational sports go together like beer and inactivity, only you tend to move around slightly more. It's one thing to sit in front of the TV and suck down a few beers—it's quite another to get out there and put your doughy body on the line. Here are some faves:

Softball

This is the ultimate sport for beer drinkers. No one will bat an eye if you drink the entire time the game is being played—just so long as you don't spill. You want to take your raps while swigging Bud from a Big Gulp cup? No problem, just don't slosh any of it on the catcher.

Caution: If you're not drinking while you play, you *will* begin to feel like you don't belong. Any guy who doesn't have a mustache, or still has a discernable jawline between his neck and face, will probably feel the same way.

Pool

This is another sport popular with folks who like to nurse a drink during competition. Whether it's billiards, bumper pool, or snooker, they're generally favored by people who eschew sun and sky for a dark bar, slightly overcast with a cancerous cloud of cigarette smoke. Playing pool is also a great way to kill time while the woman you're working on slowly gets looped.

Basketball

Not the full-court game. Not even the half-court game. Nope, if there's any beer drinking with real basketball, it's only *after* the game has been played. We're talking about Pop-A-Shot Basketball. Probably the most popular game in any sports bar. It's a small, enclosed free throw game. You stand about eight feet from the basket with half a dozen small-size basketballs in front of you. You've got forty seconds to get as many baskets as you can.

Again, it looks pretty cool if you're drinking a beer and can pull this off one-handed. Can't really be much of a challenge to get to that level though, because I swear to God, I've never seen a black guy play this game.

Darts

Every pub, Irish bar, and sleazy dive has a dartboard. The general rule of thumb is, "If there's no seat on the toilet, there's a dartboard on the wall." But where is the athlete? They only come out at night. The lowest on the beer sports ladder: the Dart Player.

Fact: There has never in history been a dart player worth a shit that didn't eventually become a pathetic alcoholic. That's because to get any good at this "sport" takes years, and the only place on earth outside of a county fair that anyone has *ever* thrown a dart is in dive bars with shitty jukeboxes.

But don't worry, you won't be able to hear the music over the 90-decibel roar that drunk dart tossers are famous for. You can't really discern what they're shouting about, save for the occasional blurts of "Oh!" "Ha!" and "Ooh!" Dart players shout more monosyllabic crap than a roomful of retards fighting over a fish stick. The one sound you *want* to hear is "Ow!" from a degenerate dart hurler getting hit in the eye. But alas, it never comes.

Foosball

Puh-leaze. How can you possibly drink a beer when you need both hands to work those "man-poles"? And yes, that's *exactly* how gay this "sport" is. Big thumbs down on this one. Americans don't like *real* soccer, why the hell would we take an interest in this midget version? Actually that's a disservice to midgets, because next to robots and monkeys, they're one of the funniest things around. The only thing Foosball is good for is ramming one of the handles into the nuts of the guy across the table.

Golf

Golf is another great way to piss away several hours in the sun getting liquor blistered with a few buddies. Perhaps the only way to improve the game would be to get rid of the whole "hit the ball into the hole with the clubs" thing. Then we'd never have to get out of the cart. We'd just drive around on the grass, drinking beer after beer, cracking jokes about one another being a fruit. Bliss.

MAN-O-VATION:
PRO-DRIVE SAFETY CART

Any duffer will tell you, you need a really good driver. As the driver of the golf cart, passenger safety is *your* responsibility. Here's a simple device to allow you to keep both hands on the steering wheel when you're out on the links:

The Safety Cart's greatest safety feature is the pony keg mounted to the back, hooked to a copper tube that runs right to the driver's mouth, leaving both his hands free to hold the wheel for responsible driving.

The keg is kept at constant pressure every time you apply the brakes. Whether you're careening down the fairway or doing doughnuts in the sand trap, you and your passengers can relax, knowing you've got both hands on the wheel of the Pro-Drive Safety Cart.

If there is a downside, it's that the Safety Cart eliminates the numerous empties you'd have from bringing a twelve-pack on the course, leaving you nothing to toss into the rough.

BALLPARK BEER

That large cup of ballpark beer can be some of the worst swill you'll use to punish your kidneys. It's got everything going against it: It's usually a wimpy, light lager that's already gone flat. It's never very cold (for a crappy lager, a huge mistake) and costs more than the two hot links you'll eat with it.

But if the company is good, the wind is right, and your team doesn't blow their early lead, that same beer can be absolutely perfect. It's the ideal drink for slowly killing an afternoon, relaxing with your buddies.

But to help you prepare for that hit your wallet's gonna take, here's a list of tap beer prices for every Major League Baseball stadium. Because friends, beer, and baseball go together like hot dogs, Babe Ruth, and syphilis.

BEER PRICES AT MAJOR LEAGUE STADIUMS

Team	Ballpark	Size	Price	Price/oz.
BOSTON RED SOX	Fenway	12 oz.	$5.25	$0.44
SAN FRANCISCO GIANTS	SBC Park	14 oz.	$5.50	$0.39
HOUSTON ASTROS	Minute Maid Park	16 oz.	$6.00	$0.38
NEW YORK YANKEES	Yankee Stadium	16 oz.	$5.75	$0.36
ATLANTA BRAVES	Turner Field	16 oz.	$5.75	$0.36
OAKLAND ATHLETICS	Network Associates Coliseum	14 oz.	$5.00	$0.36
LOS ANGELES DODGERS	Dodger Stadium	20 oz.	$7.00	$0.35
SEATTLE MARINERS	Safeco Field	16 oz.	$5.50	$0.34
ANAHEIM ANGELS	Angels Stadium	16 oz.	$5.25	$0.33
COLORADO ROCKIES	Coors Field	16 oz.	$5.25	$0.33
TAMPA BAY DEVIL RAYS	Tropicana Field	16 oz.	$5.00	$0.31
ARIZONA DIAMONDBACKS	Bank One Ballpark	16 oz.	$5.00	$0.31
CLEVELAND INDIANS	Jacobs Field	14 oz.	$4.25	$0.30
NEW YORK METS	Shea Stadium	21 oz.	$6.25	$0.30
MILWAUKEE BREWERS	Miller Park	16 oz.	$4.75	$0.30
SAN DIEGO PADRES	Petco Park	20 oz.	$5.75	$0.29
MONTREAL EXPOS	Olympic Stadium	12 oz.	$3.39	$0.28
CHICAGO WHITE SOX	U.S. Cellular Field	16 oz.	$4.50	$0.28
DETROIT TIGERS	Comerica Park	16 oz.	$4.50	$0.28
CHICAGO CUBS	Wrigley Field	16 oz.	$4.50	$0.28
KANSAS CITY ROYALS	Kauffman Stadium	12 oz.	$3.25	$0.27
ST. LOUIS CARDINALS	Busch Stadium	24 oz.	$6.50	$0.27
TORONTO BLUE JAYS	Skydome	14 oz.	$3.74	$0.27
TEXAS RANGERS	The Ballpark in Arlington	20 oz.	$5.25	$0.26
FLORIDA MARLINS	Pro Player Stadium	20 oz.	$5.25	$0.26
PHILADELPHIA PHILLIES	Citizens Bank Park	21 oz.	$5.50	$0.26
CINCINNATI REDS	Great American Ballpark	20 oz.	$5.00	$0.25
PITTSBURGH PIRATES	PNC Park	16 oz.	$4.00	$0.25
BALTIMORE ORIOLES	Camden Yards	18 oz.	$4.25	$0.24
MINNESOTA TWINS	Metrodome	24 oz.	$5.50	$0.23

Best buy **MINNESOTA TWINS**   Worst buy **BOSTON RED SOX**

113

THE FASTEST BEER DRINKER EVER

How fast can you chug a beer? Ten seconds? Five seconds? How fast can you chug *three* beers? A minute? Those are all fast times. But even if you could chug nearly three beers in a minute, you'd still be about forty-six times slower than the fastest beer drinker of all time.

According to the *Guinness Book of World Records,* that title goes to Steven Petrosino, who on June 22, 1977, drank 1 liter of beer (33 ounces) in 1.3 seconds at the Gingerbreadman Bar in Carlisle, Pennsylvania.

As a twenty-five-year-old postgrad student at Penn State, Petrosino tended bar at the Gingerbreadman, where he crushed the previous record held by an Englishman by 56%, showing once again the importance of the home field advantage. Petrosino's record remained undefeated for fourteen years.

In addition to setting the record for 1 liter, Petrosino also set the records for the 1/4 liter (0.137 seconds) and the 1/2 liter (0.4 seconds). Imagine drinking a Tall Boy in less than half a second. At that rate, you'd be through a six-pack in under three seconds. With that kind of speed, you'd never have to worry about getting pulled over with open containers in your car. "Honest, Officer, I was just taking these cans to the recycling center."

In 1991 Petrosino's amazing time became a permanent undefeated record when Guinness removed all records for beer and booze consumption from their famed book. As of January 2004, his record remains unbroken.

The great Steven Petrosino's monumental achievements stand like the beer equivalent of "most career home runs" and "most single season home runs" combined. And these triumphant records will no doubt stand for a very long time . . . until some black guy inevitably comes along and smashes them.

IN MEMORIAM: THE FOX

Most of us have never seen Steve Petrosino display his incredible drinking skill. However, longtime *Man Show* fans did get a chance to witness The Fox, whose speed and dexterity have made him somewhat of a Barry Bonds to Petrosino's Babe Ruth.

It's been said The Fox could drink a beer faster than most men could spill it on the floor. But the truth is, The Fox probably would have drunk the spilled beer before it hit the floor as well, because he would have been standing on his head.

Though he's no longer with us, we remember The Fox, both for his power-drinking prowess and for the laughs he brought to the *Man Show* with his "good time" spirit.

To The Fox!

FISHING

It's six in the morning and you're sitting on the muddy shore of a remote lake with a jar of leeches next to you. That means either the breakup was really bad, or you've gone fishing. Whether you fish on the shore or from a boat, beer is every bit as important to the experience as your pole and bait.

You could fish by yourself and drink all that beer alone, but it's better to do it with a friend, because he can keep an eye out for the game warden while you drain the vein. No leak is worth a $356 fine and a desk appearance. And you *are* gonna piss, because the number of beers you drink usually exceeds the number of fish you catch—and so it should, or you just didn't bring enough beer, you *idiot.*

Go ahead and get drunk. The only time a fish even has a fighting chance is when you're so messed up that you and your buddy are wrestling in the mud because he thought it would be funny to drop a leech down your plumber crack. Ah, memories . . .

And if the fish gets away? There are always more fish. In fact you don't even have to like fish to enjoy fishing. You can just throw them back. That's why a fishing trip is highly recommended for anyone who A) likes beer and B) has at least one friend. The same goes for camping, which is really just fishing without the worms and water.

But if you're going to fish, you're going to need to make it legal. Here's a breakdown, by state, of the cost of a fishing license.

NONRESIDENT FRESHWATER FISHING LICENSE FEES

State	Annual	5-Day	3-Day	State	Annual	5-Day	3-Day
ALABAMA	$31.00	$8.00	$5.00	N.H.	$53.00	$25.00	$15.00
ALASKA	$100.00	$21.50	$13.00	NEW JERSEY	$34.00	$14.00	$8.50
ARIZONA	$51.50	$21.00	$13.00	NEW MEXICO	$44.00	$21.00	$13.00
ARKANSAS	$32.00	$12.50	$5.00	NEW YORK	$40.00	$18.00	$11.00
CALIFORNIA	$82.45	$11.00	$5.00	N. CAROLINA	$30.00	$25.00	$15.00
COLORADO	$40.25	$18.25	$11.00	N. DAKOTA	$27.00	$11.00	$5.00
CONN.	$40.00	$27.00	$16.00	OHIO	$24.00	$15.00	$9.00
DELAWARE	$15.00	$7.50	$5.00	OKLAHOMA	$37.00	$18.50	$11.50
FLORIDA	$31.50	$12.00	$5.00	OREGON	$65.00	$25.00	$15.00
GEORGIA	$24.00	$17.50	$10.50	PENN.	$35.00	$21.50	$13.00
HAWAII	$25.00	$7.50	$5.00	R.I.	$31.00	$27.00	$16.00
IDAHO	$74.50	$26.50	$18.50	S. CAROLINA	$35.00	$8.00	$5.00
ILLINOIS	$24.50	$9.50	$7.50	S. DAKOTA	$59.00	$50.00	$30.00
INDIANA	$24.75	$9.00	$5.00	TENNESSEE	$51.00	$34.00	$20.50
IOWA	$36.50	$20.00	$12.00	TEXAS	$30.00	$20.00	$12.00
KANSAS	$40.50	$20.50	$12.50	UTAH	$70.00	$23.00	$14.00
KENTUCKY	$35.00	$25.00	$21.00	VERMONT	$41.00	$33.50	$20.00
LOUISIANA	$60.00	$19.00	$11.50	VIRGINIA	$30.00	$7.50	$7.50
MAINE	$50.00	$24.00	$21.00	WASHINGTON	$43.80	$16.50	$10.00
MARYLAND	$40.00	$14.00	$4.00	W. VIRGINIA	$40.00	$25.00	$15.00
MASS.	$37.50	$30.00	$23.50	WISCONSIN	$34.00	$19.00	$11.25
MICHIGAN	$31.00	$28.00	$21.00	WYOMING	$65.00	$50.00	$30.00
MINNESOTA	$35.00	$18.00	$11.00	WASH., D.C.	$10.00	$7.50	$5.00
MISSISSIPPI	$33.00	$28.00	$17.00				
MISSOURI	$35.00	$25.00	$15.00				
MONTANA	$67.00	$55.00	$33.00				
NEBRASKA	$45.00	$28.00	$14.00				
NEVADA	$51.00	$28.00	$20.00				

And please, be a Man, pick up your empties. It's one thing to give the fish a golden shower—it's quite another to leave a mess behind for the next guy.

Source: http://www.dnr.state.md.us/service/fishingcost.html

THE GREATEST BEER TALE EVER TOLD

Back when they were playing football for the Philadelphia Eagles, linebacker Tim Rossovich and tight end Mike Ditka had a contest to see who could open more beer bottles with their teeth. Some people—I call them "women"—wonder why anyone would ever challenge somebody to such a retarded contest. If you're a Man, however, the question doesn't require an answer. But for the benefit of you little ladies out there who might be reading this book instead of scrubbing floors or gossiping at the fence with the neighbor you secretly hate, here's the skinny.

A *gentleman's challenge,* such as "who can open more beers with his teeth?" is actually an archetypal test of another man's character. This seemingly self-destructive contest helps a guy learn another man's abilities, and more important, his limitations. Knowing how many bottle caps someone can pry off with their teeth answers the great questions one might have about another man: Is he someone you'd want in your foxhole during combat? Can he be trusted around your girlfriend? Is he as dumb as he looks?

As a dramatic date with destiny, this epic competition between Rossovich and Ditka has taken on the grandeur and scale of the greatest American tall tales: John Henry, Paul Bunyan, Pecos Bill, and John "The Wadd" Holmes. But instead of Man v. Machine or Man v. 14,000 Vaginas, this would be that greatest duel of them all: Man v. Man.

Rossovich and Ditka tore into their bottles. Their strategies were simple. Rossovich, eschewing form for speed, took off like a sprinter, tearing into the first bottle with teeth of fury. Ditka, ever the marathoner, paced himself evenly, intending to save his energy for an explosive burst of scattering enamel at the finish line.

As each man hooked a bottle cap on his lower incisors, they intently eyed the other from across their makeshift battlefield. Two men had entered this arena as mere mortals, but one would emerge a god.

Rossovich was brash. It seemed he didn't even bite down on the top of the cap. It was as if he was only striking his lower teeth with the top of the bottle, sending the cap into the air with a chilling *CLACK!* He alternated hands; as one crashed a bottle against the teeth like a mighty steam hammer, the other plunged into the waiting beers, grasping for the next bottle whose moment to become part of history had finally arrived.

But Ditka gazed at his foe with the cold, calculated, insolent patience of a lab monkey, who silently waits for the instant the animal rescue hippie chick foolishly opens his cage, releasing the terror of his flesh-ripping fury on her un-madeup face.

Ditka's hands steadily grasped every bottle with the firm assuredness of a fireman pulling a toddler out of a well. Each cold scrape of unyielding metal against his jagged lower teeth rattled his jaw and rang throughout his skull. His head would fill with the sound of each thunderous clang. Yet the deafening echo was but a whisper compared to the heavenly chant, from within his heart, that rose above the cacophony in his head. "Win Mike . . . Win Mike . . . Win Mike . . . I'm not gay . . . Win Mike . . ."

CLACK! CLACK! CLACK! Rossovich worked his bottles.

NnnnnnnNnNnNnNNNNNNGGGGGGAAAAAGGGGHHHH! Ditka tore another cap free.

It was as if the trials of Hercules were wrought double. Each of these mythic supermen was at the top of his game. As physical specimens, they would never again achieve such heights. But from here, they would both begin their divergent paths into the latter half of their legacies. One would have to slowly fade from men's minds into the haze of obscurity, the other would mount his steady ascent into the pantheon of heroes about whom other men would sing.

Victory would grace only the man who proved he wanted it more. This man, whose 110% would somehow defy all mathematical possibility and generate one or two percent more, would singularly taste triumph in the blood filling his mouth.

Which titan possessed the lead was hard to tell until the very end. But when one man slowly fell silent, it was Rossovich who could still be heard clacking glass and steel against his teeth and lips. The mighty Ditka had given it his all, and lost.

Legend has it that when the steel-driving John Henry drove home his final spike, he wearily laid down his hammer and died. But Ditka, the mighty Ditka, would have no such fabled ending. Weakened, he watched as Rossovich mechanically stripped more virgin bottles of their seals. He did not stop for some time. Ditka could only watch in disgrace. Savoring his victory, Rossovich began drinking the topless beers. Finally, as if to crush the last bones of his vanquished opponent, he began to take bites from the bottles and chew the glass.

When it was over, one could sense how the tale of this competition would be spun in somber, hushed tones to the children of generations to come. They would listen, certain that it couldn't be so, but the heroic Ditka had lost 100-3.

Despite how it seems, Tim Rossovich was not a sore winner. Crunching glass was something he'd done for years. But after opening, drinking, and chewing the better part of a hundred bottles, he'd learned exactly what kind of man Ditka was. And that he must never let him near his girlfriend.

Based on an actual event as reported in **Sports Illustrated,** ***September 20, 1971.***

MAN-O-VATIONS

Gadgets are essential

to the evolution of Man. From the time he put a twig in an ant nest to rustle up his lunch, to moments later when he used the same twig to fish something out of a McDonald's Dumpster, he has cleverly designed tools and inventions to improve his life.

Long a fixture on the *Man Show,* "Man-o-Vations" puts forward the best technology has to offer to make your life more complete. Presented here are Man-o-Vations that make beer drinking easier, faster, safer, and most important, *Manly.*

The Man Show Industries and its foreign subsidiaries shall assume no responsibility for any injuries incurred while some dumbass uses these Man-o-Vations, up to and including dismemberment or death.

PARTY PAL

Every time you throw a party at your house, the same thing happens. Your drunken friends, with their lousy aim, leave a splashy puddle of urine on your bathroom floor. Isn't there something that can prevent this mess?

Say hello to the Party Pal piss puller!

123

Designed in Europe by Germany's leading urine extraction specialists, this urine extraction system is guaranteed to keep your floors dry and your guests happy.

At the top of its neck—heated to a warm 99.4 degrees—is a patented suction device featuring a velvet-smooth orifice that engulfs your guest's penis, forming a moist yet urine-tight seal.

Then, much like a dairy cow, in no time at all, your guest is milked of blast after blast of all his scalding-hot urine. While the whole process can take less than a minute, the Party Pal has adjustable speeds so your guest can induce a slow but rhythmic swallowing motion that takes its time to work your guest's penis until it explodes like a frothy hose.

The powerful sucking of the Party Pal is so strong that even if he wanted to hold back, your guest would go weak at the knees and uncontrollably send gush after monumental gush of his molten fluids down the throat of the insatiable device. The Party Pal then chokes down each and every hot drop of man mist from the depths of his low-hanging bladder.

Once he is drained, your guest will simply extract his penis from its dripping mouth, wiping any excess on its neck, turn and walk away. He will, no doubt, tell all the other guys about the Party Pal, so that each and every hanging penis at the party takes its turn dumping a splashing load of salty urine down the hungry gullet of the Party Pal piss puller!

Available in both Frat House and House Party sizes.

FRIGI-CHAIR

Since the Dawn of Man, when he would sit in his cave gazing at shadows cast upon the wall by firelight, the male species has dreamed of having the perfect chair in which to sit while He contemplates the nature of His reality.

Now, at the dawn of this new millennium, Man has at last arrived at this dream. Behold the new Frigi-Chair, the "Ultimate 21st Century Television Seating Device" designed exclusively for beer enthusiasts!

In this chair, Man is finally free to observe and ponder His reality and break wind without interruption as He's warmed by the alcohol He's poured into His body.

Each padded vinyl Frigi-Chair has a 2500-watt refrigerator housed inside the seat that keeps beer icy cold.* Now you'll never miss another minute of the ball game or the *Man Show* because you had to run to the kitchen for another cold one. There's a refrigerator with a two-case capacity right beneath you![+]

Each Frigi-Chair comes with a special remote that, with a push of a button, pops a fresh beer through the armrest right into your hand![±] Inside the remote is housed a bottle opener so you need not get up ever again.

Don't be fooled by imitations. Only the Frigi-Chair comes with the handy Cap Catcher (patent pending) on the side for bottle caps, all for slightly more than the price of a chair and a refrigerator.[x]

* *Caution: Chair does NOT recline. Any attempt to do so will result in severe electric shock.*

[+] *A three-case capacity model is available if you have a wife or girlfriend who watches* Charmed *for an additional $32.*

[±] *Left-hand models available for a nominal additional cost of $485.*

[x] *Based on prices of refrigerators and chairs as found in the Microsoft/Time Warner/ Montgomery Ward Winter Catalog 2024*

BAR BUDDY GLOVE

It's long been known that the bowls of peanuts and pretzels at the local bar are often teeming with germs. The culprit? Guys who didn't wash their hands after drawing draughts from the trouser taps in the bathroom. They reach into the bowls of pretzels, soiling the contents with urine and fecal matter still on their hands. Disgusting!

But you won't have to worry about that anymore, thanks to the Bar Buddy Glove. Each glove is made of surgical latex that forms a sanitary barrier between the piss-soaked pretzels and your hands.

With the Bar Buddy Glove you can gobble down mouthful after salty mouthful of peanuts tainted with human waste without the gnawing fear of getting any on your hands.

Not available in left-hand model.

BEER GUARD

In this modern age, staying ahead in the practical joke wars requires the latest technology. If you want to keep a friend from pissing in your beer, you're gonna have to keep up. With bigger and bigger bottles, and smaller and small penises flooding the market, it's become too easy for friends and strangers to drain their vein in your domestic draft. How will you know if a friend has peed in your beer?

With the Beer Guard Test Kit you'll be able to find out.

Each kit comes complete with a book of litmus paper specially designed to measure ammonia and salt levels that can verify within 97% accuracy whether someone has let their snake squirt in your Sam Adams.

Just rub the paper on the top of the bottle, can, or glass and wait fifteen seconds. If the paper turns blue, your beer is untainted. But if it turns a slightly darker shade of blue, someone has bathed his bone in your Budweiser.

Luckily the kit also comes with a NASA-approved, vacuum-sealed, clinically sterile, titanium box that holds a supply of forty-eight beer-flavored tablets that can return your drink to its previous flavor for full enjoyment.

Know what you're drinking. Get a Beer Guard.

BAR-CADE GAME

Tired of playing the same old pinball and video poker at your local bar? Here at last is something designed for people with .10 or more blood alcohol level. It's the After Hours Driving Simulator, from Drunktronix. It's just like a car simulator, only you can actually get drunk while driving!

Pound that beer and take the wheel! With the latest in today's digital simulation technology, you can at last mix *fake* driving with *real* drinking!

Relive the drunk driving glories of yesteryear. Experience the delight of blazing down a street in a blackout without the fear of consequences. Just like Dad used to do! Once again, you can feel the excitement of running a red light, as you puke on the realistic passenger seat.

Hey, watch out for that Mother Against Drunk Driving up ahead in the road— oops! She'll never walk again. And you've just scored a hundred and fifty points! Time for another beer!

Thanks to the internal cable modem, you can drive to *another* simulated bar for last call! Get there too late? No problem, drink a *real* beer in their simulated parking lot!

Now tear ass back home, because you've got to take the kids to school. Look out! Was that a dog or a bum? Who cares? More beer!

The Drunktronix After Hours Driving Simulator—a great way to have fun before your drive home from the bar.

The Drunktronix After Hours Driving Simulator is strictly for entertainment purposes and should not be used for wagering.

BELLY BLEND BODYSUIT

Beach ball beer gut get you down? Are you tired of the unwanted fat rolls on your stomach extending way too far past your chest? Then you need to get the Belly Blend Bodysuit. The *only* stomach-concealing suit sanctioned by both the Motorcycle Division of the Boston Police and the LPGA.

131

Made of new Lycra-Ion, the Belly Blend Bodysuit has extra padding in the chest, shoulders, and arms, blending the rest of your body in with your distended belly. Your chest will now evenly flow into your unpadded gut, giving you the natural contour of a bodybuilder teeming with performance-enhancing compounds!

Each pad is actually a poly-resin acrylic bag filled with *real* human fat, retrieved from the most exclusive liposculpture clinics throughout greater Miami. We collect all the discarded biomass, fashion it into stylish padding, and pass the savings on to you.

Why go to a gym, when you can keep your beer gut and still look great! Get your Belly Blend Bodysuit today!

The Belly Blend Bodysuit is proudly made in the USA. Results may vary.

CAR CAN CRUSHER

Is that pile of empty beer cans in your backseat starting to obstruct your rearview mirror? Is it becoming impossible for you to monitor the smoky exhaust through your back window? Did you know smoky exhaust is one of the leading causes of liver damage in laboratory mice that live near the freeway?

Well, now you can get that pile of beer cans under control and out of your rearview, making it possible to once again observe that oily black cloud coming out your tailpipe—thanks to the Car Can Crusher.

Linking into what's left of your car's existing hydraulics system, the Car Can Crusher sits in your backseat and delivers a mammoth 14 lbs. psi, to flatten both twelve-ounce *and* Tall Boy cans. Each can is then jettisoned out the patented Disposal Slot you cut into your trunk, allowing you to send that swirling metal disc flying into the traffic behind you, landing harmlessly . . . wherever.

How does the Disposal Slot system work? At high speeds, air pressure builds up at the tail of your car. Cutting a hole in your trunk just above your exhaust pipe sucks that air into the car, where it repressurizes the Can Crusher.

The can is then smashed flat before the excess pressure is used to propel the spinning aluminum wheel zinging into the streets, where it will land as harmless as a discarded, jagged CD.

And don't worry, this metal crushing behemoth can keep up with even the fastest beer chuggers and still keep your car—and your rearview—clear of debris, allowing you to keep an eye on that deadly carbon monoxide cloud!

Get the Car Can Crusher—the lab mice will thank you.

BEER'D SCIENCE

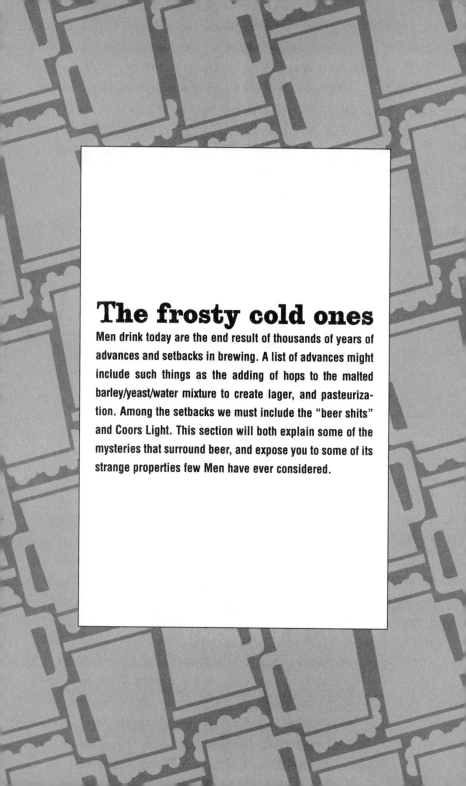

The frosty cold ones

Men drink today are the end result of thousands of years of advances and setbacks in brewing. A list of advances might include such things as the adding of hops to the malted barley/yeast/water mixture to create lager, and pasteurization. Among the setbacks we must include the "beer shits" and Coors Light. This section will both explain some of the mysteries that surround beer, and expose you to some of its strange properties few Men have ever considered.

WHY DO I FEEL DRUNK?

You feel drunk because the alcohol in your beer affects the neurons in the brain. Specifically, the alcohol is kind enough to monkey with three chemicals that are vital to getting wasted: gamma-aminobutyric acid (GABA), serotonin, and dopamine.

As neurotransmitters, these three chemicals pass between different nerve cells as signals, activating or deactivating the cells that they are targeted for, although GABA is generally a deactivator.

Alcohol tends to lead to an increase in levels of serotonin. This is a good thing because serotonin is the magical goo that makes for "happy" feelings when we booze it up. It elevates a person's mood, enabling him to laugh, sing, be funny, and for once in his life, pick up the check.

GABA, on the other hand, generally diminishes serotonin and slows the brain down, often inhibiting reflexes, muscle control, and your good sense not to talk shit about the boss.

Now, the bad news: In large quantities alcohol is a poison and can damage various organs, including the liver. Your body knows better than your brain, and immediately starts to break down the booze and pass it out your pee hole—sometimes when you're not looking. But when the quantity of alcohol consumed is too large, your body takes the keys from your brain.

The first stop on its drive is the bathroom, so you can puke. Congratulations, you just got even funnier. However, by the time you've got your face hanging into the crapper far deeper than your ass ever does, it's usually too late. You're going to have a hangover. Unless you stay drunk, that is.

Was it worth it? Well, if it weren't, you'd never drink again. And that would be a tragedy.

BEER ALGEBRA

Though beer has been around for thousands of years, many of its miraculous properties still baffle scientists. How is it that the more Men drink, the more courage we possess? It's true! Just eight or nine pints of Guinness at a company mixer gives you the amazing courage to unveil your bold plan for maximizing third quarter returns, and the incredible balls to tell your manager he's a droning jagoff.

What is it about being deep into a twelve-pack that makes your charm go off the charts? It's true! Somehow with a couple hundred ounces of Miller Lite sloshing around in his veins, the average Joe gains the swagger and panache of James Dean before his joyride in the Spyder.

And why is it that the more beer a *woman* drinks, the more interesting and accessible *she* becomes? Five or six Coronas can turn her from just another secretary with salsa under her nails into a captivating conversationalist—with stunning breasts!

All this is possible because of Beer Algebra or "Beer-gebra."

One of the basic principles of Beer-gebra is: Whatever you do to one side of an equation is balanced on the other side. For the secretary, adding six Mexican lagers to one side of the equation is the same as adding several IQ points and a cup size to the other.

But use caution when calculating such complex mathematical ratios. Too many *cervezas* to the left side of the equation may cause you to wake up, look to the right, and find your mammoth-breasted conversationalist is nothing more than a chunky receptionist with stringy hair and a bedroom filled with stuffed animals . . . again.

This is an example of an "$a^2 + b^2$ = Sneak out and pray she doesn't tell anyone" equation, found in the more advanced Swig-Onometry.

"BORN ON" DATES

Not everyone knows it, but beer is technically classified as a "food," meaning it can spoil and go bad. According to Anheuser-Busch, their beer should be consumed within 110 days of its being brewed. After that, it loses flavor. That's why megabrewers make a lot of noise about the importance of their beer's documented "born on" date.

With the dreaded scourge of spoiled beer lurking at the borders, your first question might be, "Would keeping the beer in the crisper drawer help preserve it longer?" And the answer is—this may come as an unexpected surprise—"you're an idiot."

When was the last time anyone threw away a beer because it was no longer "fresh," *ever?* Yes, beer is food, but it's not like milk. If you drink spoiled milk, you'll spend all day sitting on the shitter—enough *good* beer can make you do that. Drinking a beer that's lived beyond its expiration date is like eating leftover pizza the next day—it's still pretty damn good. And even if *you* didn't want to drink expired beer, you could at least save it for company, or your idiot brother-in-law.

There are, of course, great religious quandaries to bestowing beer with "life." Does beer have a soul? Do the darker beers have more of it than the light beers? Does a fundamentalist consider a spilled beer an abortion? Is it against God to try to extend a beer's life?

Instead of worrying about a "born on" date, shouldn't we care more about how beers "die"? I'll drink to *that.* Some beers die young. Others live until the ripe old age of thirty minutes after the boss is gone. Where does a beer go when it dies? Personally, I raise the lid, and give it a burial at sea . . . or anywhere between here and the next off ramp if I can't hold it any longer. It's very touching.

All attempts to round out the number of pages in this book aside, the importance of a beer's "born on" date deserves critical examination, beginning with the question, Who is it for?

The truth is, few people ever have beer in their fridge long enough to worry about it expiring. If you buy a six-pack of beer, you'd only have to drink one beer for every eighteen days before it risked losing flavor. If you're drinking less than two beers a month, you're not really a "beer drinker." Most likely, you don't know what a *good* beer tastes like, let alone a bad one. You might even be a pussy. You're not going to benefit from a "born on" date.

Conversely, if you buy cases and cases of beer, you're probably the kind of guy who *drinks* cases and cases. You've got bigger things to worry about besides when your beer was born, like "When's that next disability check ever gonna show up?"

So if the casual drinker and the heavy drinker don't need a "born on" date, who does? Certainly not store owners. They don't keep beer on their shelves long enough to care, because they know what does and doesn't sell in their 'hood. If it doesn't sell, they won't stock it. They're in business to sell beer, not store it.

So who benefits from all the hoopla about "born on" dates? Could it be that pimping a beer's "born on" date is just another marketing scam? Is it perhaps nothing more than a ploy by piss beer companies that annually spend more on advertising than they do on hops? You already know the answer.

The only guys who give a rat's ass about things like "born on" dates and "cold filtering" and "beechwood aging" are the same chumps who actually believe they can burn fat while they sleep, or add up to three inches without creams or pills. I'm not falling for that again. The best method to keep beer from going bad is to use the same one the Egyptians used: Drink it.

THE MYSTERIOUS BEER-PIZZA NEXUS

Much like Lincoln had a secretary named Kennedy, and Kennedy had a secretary named Lincoln, there is a strange series of coincidences and characteristics that link a beer and a slice of pizza.

The most obvious connection is that both are best when shared by friends. But did you know that both beer and pizza together reportedly once stopped Louie Anderson from eating that gray thing in his fridge? It's eerie. Here's a list of odd yet magical things that form a strange link between a beer and a slice of pizza:

They taste great when cold.

They have the same amount of carbs.

People fight over the last one.

You try to down as many as you can.

Six of them oughta do ya just 'bout right.

In New York, cops get them for free.

They make a great breakfast.

They both give you power over the homeless.

Both are no longer allowed in the delivery room.

Both go great on a fat girl.

They can liven up any funeral.

Neither should ever be made by Asians.

Either one costs about a buck, if you can just get it out of your kid's piggybank.

Both can make a lesbian's day.

They each leave your other hand free to steer . . . and shoot.

Either one makes a great "last meal."

Have enough of them, and you'll get yourself a nice pair of boobs.

Both can quiet a baby down.

Perhaps the most enigmatic of all the links shared by beer and pizza is this peculiar fact: The night before his fateful trip to Dallas, Jack *Kennedy* shared *pizza* and a *beer* with a hooker in the *Lincoln* bedroom. Simply chilling.

TROUBLE IN PARADISE

It's been all fun

and games up to now. You've had over a hundred pages celebrating the one friend that most of you will have for the rest of your life. But any book that spends so much time, while you're taking a dump, extolling the virtues and joys that go with beer should also be responsible and cast light upon its downsides . . . and make fun of anyone who suffers from them.

DO I HAVE A DRINKING PROBLEM?

Yikes! That's never fun to consider. A drinking problem can be devastating to a beer lover. You don't want to become one of those poor slobs who has to drink non-alcoholic beer. Have you ever tasted one of those things? But the question deserves serious consideration. Here's a little story:

"Tom Johnson" is a student at a small Midwestern college. One night he attends a party at another student's dorm. Like any good friend, Tom valiantly tries to help empty the keg. Sometime after placing second in the belching contest, he wanders off. It's 4 AM and the urge to spontaneously sleep has finally caught up with him. He judiciously decides to bed down for the night in the doorjamb leading to the hallway. About twenty minutes into his blissful slumber, Tom expels his share of the keg from his bladder. The warm liquid is quietly absorbed by his pants, shirt, and the carpet.

Early the next morning, Tom slowly wakes, or as they say in the medical profession, he "comes to." The first thing he notices is how sore his neck is; the second, how cold and damp his parachute pants are. He takes a moment to get a grip on what's happened. Suddenly, the meaning of that odd smell becomes all too clear. Someone must have peed on him while he was sleeping again! But this time, he's wrong. As anyone can tell, Tom is in denial. Though he may not be able to admit it, the signs are clear to the impartial observer. Our little scholar, Tom, has a *urine* problem.

Each year thousands of cases of Passive Intermittent Soaking Syndrome like Tom's get misdiagnosed as a drinking problem. Luckily, thanks to Tom's voluminous beer drinking, the signs were caught early. Now, through the help of adult diapers with an 87% absorption rate, Tom's condition is almost undetectable.

The next time someone tells you that you have a drinking problem, get checked for PISS.

HANGOVERS

First of all, stop looking for a miracle cure—a pill or a wonder drink that's gonna make the pain go away. It doesn't exist, and you don't deserve one. You drank the beer and it made you its bitch. Quit crying and take it like a man. If you were drinking to get hammered, then you were playing with the house's money. And the house always wins.

Everyone has a cure for a hangover, and mine is: Don't get one. Whether you're drinking beer or real booze, it doesn't matter, you can drink to the point of criminality and still avoid the dreaded hangover. How? First, a few words about what makes a hangover.

With the standard hangover, you feel like you've been trampled in a disco fire. Maybe you were. But the point is you wake up with a dry mouth and a splitting headache. It feels like heatstroke. And that's because your body is severely dehydrated. You've been drowning your cortex in Coronas and now your brain is telling you *"agua por favor,"* which is how drunk Mexican brains say "gimme some water."

How do you keep this from happening? Drink water the night before. A lot. If you're power drinking, down a water every second or third drink. It never fails. You'll piss a lot more, but it beats the pissing and moaning you'd be doing the next morning. But are you going to listen? No. So flip around in this book for hangover "cures" that other knuckleheads use.

BEER-LIGERENCE

Drinking changes people. Some guys drink a few beers and they feel great, their spirits are high. But a few rounds later, that same guy wants to kick everybody's ass. He doesn't like the way somebody bumped him. He doesn't like the way somebody looked at him. His pussy team just lost the Series to the Arizona Diamondbacks. If a dude is a ticking time bomb, beer can be just the thing to set him off. Let's face it, if you're walking back to your car some night and you come upon two guys rolling on the ground punching each other, and one of them has fresh bite marks on his forehead, it's a pretty safe bet *someone's* been drinking.

And the fact is, nobody fights better when they're drunk, they just fight *more.* The only thing being drunk can do for you in a fight is make you impervious to pain—for a few hours. Sometime later your head hurts from the blows, your knuckles hurt from the punching, and your wrists hurt from the handcuffs. Apparently telling the cop that you pay his salary *doesn't* keep you from spending your night back at his "office" sleeping on a hard bench without your shoes. You probably shouldn't have called him "fag."

You might wonder if beer is to blame. Is there something truly evil in the brew that makes men lash out with violence? If you ask anyone with years of experience with the subconscious motivation to the overt aggression dynamic (psychologists, doctors, and bartenders), they'll tell you the root cause of every single drunken fight that's ever happened is—you guessed it—some chick.

Either she was flirting with somebody, or she *wasn't* flirting with somebody. Or a dude has a woman at home who won't fuck him, or some guy *doesn't* have a woman at home who won't fuck him. Women have got us coming and going. Maybe the question should be, Is there something truly evil in women that makes guys fight? But that could just be the beer talking.

Until Men get this whole "chicks + booze = violence" thing worked out, never, under any circumstances, drink beer out of anything made from aluminum. You don't want to bring a *can* to a *bottle* fight. That's the Chicago way.

WHAT'S UP CHUCK?

I f you're tired of barfing, puking, horking, yakking, and experiencing "deja food," give these a try. It's still tossing your cookies, but it sounds a lot more colorful.

Verb

1. Re-do lunch

2. Send a memo

3. Park 'n' bark

4. Work the abs

5. Do some Karen Carpentry

Noun

1. Supermodel Soundoff

2. Gastro Blast

3. Megabite Upload

4. Soup of the Night

5. Liquid Laugh

MAN-O-VATION:
SHAMELESS SHIRT

Sure, it's funny when someone barfs at a party. In fact the wider the spray of corn chips and Mickey's Big Mouth, the funnier it is. But what if *you're* that guy? Maybe you weren't going for laughs. Maybe you're hitting on a girl. Well, you were until you painted your pecs with puke puree.

149

That will never happen again, thanks to the new prestained Shameless Shirt. Each shirt is an explosion of vomit patterns modeled after garments taken directly from the Nick Nolte collection.

Now when you experience an alcohol avalanche in the middle of your smooth rap, you won't have to walk away, dripping with disgrace. The Shameless Shirt keeps your stinking "street pizza" a secret, so you can close the deal with the big-boned gals at the party.

Made of 100% cotton, and liberally splashed with Hurlon™, a space age miracle fiber made of gastric liquids and epoxy resins, the new Shameless Shirt makes even the biggest "mouth diarrhea" splatters blend right in. It looks so real you'll say, "Wow, I can't believe it's not puke . . . yet."

Available in two sizes: Large and Extra Chunky.

IT COULD BE WORSE

It doesn't seem possible, but when a Man has had too much beer, there are worse things that can come out of his mouth than puke. By far, the worst stuff that will ever come out of your drunken maw are *words.* Here is a list of key expressions that you must resist saying, no matter what the beer is telling you.

"Bartender, drinks are on me!"

"What the fuck are you lookin' at?"

". . . And you're *sure* that's not herpes?"

"I'll bet I can pee out that window while I'm driving."

"Yankees suck!"

"You mean you *never* seen anyone catch a lawn dart with his teeth?"

"Oh, yeah? Why don't you just take that badge off, and we'll see how tough you are."

"Maybe it'll bite me and maybe it won't, but I'm putting my cock in it."

"Okay, I *see* the train, but I can make it."

"Whattup, my niggers?"

"Don't worry, it's not loaded."

"Last one to take off his clothes and jump from the roof into the pool, that may or may not have water in it but it's too dark to tell, is a rotten egg!"

"I do."

SO, BEER MADE YOU FAT . . .

When it comes to body types, the commonly held perception is that *fat = bad.* At a very young age, we learn from the media that *chunky = no one will ever fuck me.* If you were to check with our most prestigious universities, you'd be hard-pressed to find a freshman with a finger down her throat who doesn't know that *plump = mom and dad won't love me.*

But if you examine the actual evidence, you'll find being fat is the surest path to love. In fact, after much testing, the only scientifically proven downside to being fat is that you're the first one to be eaten when the jet crashes into a mountain. But what are the odds? Other than that, being fat is all gravy, which should make you feel good. Behold the good word . . .

If you're a fat guy, you get to drink *more* beer than everyone else at the comic book fair because of your greater body mass. Most guys crap out and hit a point where they have to stop drinking; somewhere between six and twenty-seven beers. *You* can keep drinking long after everyone else has passed out asleep . . . then creep into the kitchen and drink that chocolate sauce straight from the bottle!

You know what else? America *loves* fat people. What, don't believe me? Did you ever notice how your eyes water up whenever a fat celebrity dies? Here are some names: John Belushi, Chris Farley, John Candy, Oliver Hardy, Fatty Arbuckle, Porky Pig, Orson Welles, Junior Samples, Jesus, and in about six months, John Goodman. How's that? Dry your eyes, you're crying in your beer.

Maybe you're thinking, "The only reason anyone loves them is because they're celebrities." Guess again. Here's a test: A skinny guy and a really fat guy both fall into a pit of spikes. Who do you feel more sorry for? Exactly.

So the next time you're contemplating having that ninth beer and you start to worry, *God, I'm getting fat! I'm going to become obese and no one will ever want to screw me unless I pay them . . . plus I need to get a job,* just relax. Drink that beer and know that love awaits you. The only thing you really need to worry about is where the hell you're ever gonna find a pit of spikes.

BEER TITS

To many, a pronounced beer belly is considered an achievement. Something to take pride in, to compare. A way to proudly say to the world, "Hey, I drink too much beer!" Yet for some, the beer belly is but a dream. Because in some men, their body decides to store all those beer-derived energy reserves in their boobs.

They go by several names—beer tits, man tits, beer boobs, or bitch tits—but they all carry the same shame. Strange, when you consider one of the few things that men love more than beer is a set of tits. But when you combine the two, you're left with two hairy hooters that go unloved. All across this great land are men who wish just *once* they could have sex without wearing a T-shirt.

True, some men embrace their squishy sweater kittens. Usually they can be found doing clownish cannonballs into the pool. Everyone has a chuckle, and for one brief moment the guy with the sagging sudsbags is freed from his private humiliation.

But once the splashes are over, and these guys climb out of the water, they know in their overtaxed hearts they must distract everyone from their malty mammories. And *that's* why they make their plaid trunks hang halfway off their mottled asses. After that, they got nothing. So, as they simultaneously pull their suits back up over their hairy flesh canyons, and wipe the snot dripping from their noses, they try their best to lower their high-pitched voices as they ask for another Bud. And so the charade continues.

This is the classic Beer Tits Shame Spiral: tits, pain, more beer, more tits, more pain, more beer, bigger tits . . . Shouldn't we, as beer lovers, reach out to our brothers and give comfort? Isn't it time we celebrate beer tits, as we do beer bellies? Can't we relieve these men, who through some cruel spin of the hereditary wheel store twelve-packs in their tits, from this torture? Can't we? Yes, we *can* . . . but they're just too damn funny-looking.

TEENAGERS & BEER

People talk a lot about the problem of teen drinking. Today, the only problem a fourteen-year-old has with drinking is when it clashes with the Ecstasy he took two hours ago. For teens, there has never been a problem getting beer. How do they get it? The same way you did: shoplifting.

When you're thirteen years old, one of the easiest ways to get beer is to boost it from a convenience store. Four or five of your friends enter the store and create a distraction; you grab a twelve-pack and boogie out the door during the mayhem. What could be easier? As long as the guy behind the counter with the Glock tucked under the *Penthouse* doesn't perforate you like that kid who tried stealing orange juice, you and your pals will get two or three beers apiece.

That's why most teens have to turn to adults like you for help.

It's a familiar scenario: You're walking toward the entrance of a local liquor store or market and suddenly you're approached by a pimple-faced teen. He asks if you'll take his money and buy him some beer. At that moment you fondly remember your own youthful beer-quest escapades: how your nerves churned your stomach as you approached your mark; how you bargained with the adult, promising him two cans out of the twelve-pack; and the feeling of criminal glee as you headed back to the schoolyard to get drunk.

So you listen to the kid, paying careful attention to what he wants you to buy. He wants MGD, but you decide to impart a valuable lesson to him. You say, "Life's too short for shitty beer, get some Bass or Sam Adams." You tell him you'll get a bottle opener as well. He hands you the money and you enter the store.

As you walk to the beer coolers in the back, you realize that a torch is about to be passed to a new generation. Ten or fifteen years earlier, a man much as yourself walked into a store to get you your coveted six-pack of Stroh's.

You open the door and pick up a six-pack of Bass. "Ah, what the hell." You remove three of the bottles and replace them with a trio of Sam Adams. Life *is* too short.

At the counter, you lay out the kid's money and the Korean guy asks, "Anything else?" Suddenly you remember. "Shit! Almost forgot. I told the kid I'd get a bottle opener." You take the opener and the change. The deal is done. You then pick up the beer that the kid in the parking lot is eagerly awaiting, and walk out the back door, never to see him again.

No problem.

154

BEER & MONKEYS

Don't freak out. Just remember that we're on the top of the evolutionary chain for a reason. Yes, they're ugly drunks and possess deadly accuracy with their feces, but be firm with your monkey. Say as evenly as you can, "All right, Gary, give me back my beer. . . . Give me back my beer." And *never* break eye contact, because in his world that's a sign of submission and, as an instinctual killer, your beer-crazed monkey will not hesitate to bite your face and mouth without remorse.

He's still not giving it back? Keep on him. You cannot be afraid to use the one thing that makes us superior to him.

"What's that?"

What do you mean, "What's that?" Surely you know what it is that makes us superior to that screeching monkey who won't give back your beer. It's the power of speech. Language. Unlike what Gary's doing right now, you don't have to go all pop-eyed and gnash your teeth to communicate a desire. You have the powers of speech and language, the innate ability to put cognitive thought into a medium for others to receive and understand.

"Huh?"

We can *talk* to each other. And your little monkey friend fears it.

"Oh, right. Okay, I'll try it . . . [to monkey] All right, Gary, give me back my beer. . . ."

See, he's confused. The words confuse him.

"C'mon, Gary . . . give it back."

Make no sudden moves.

"Give it back and I'll get you a nice banana."

No!! He fears language, but don't *bargain* with him!

"That's a nice monkey . . . give it back."

Don't break eye contact. His wide-open mouth of sharp teeth means it's working.

"Niiiice monkey . . . niiice Gaaarrrry . . ."

Easy . . . Keep talking to him . . . Remember the Force—of *Speech.*

"Riiiiight, the Force—of Speech."

Now reach for that beer and use the Force.

"Fucking monkey, gimme my beer! Yeah, you heard me right, I said 'fucking monkey'; you're the one with the diaper. Now hand it over."

Hey, take it easy. Don't piss him off. You just want your beer back.

"Fuck the beer. This isn't about beer anymore. This is about me and that bitch ass, non-evolved Darwinian also-ran."

Fool! He's a *monkey,* not some stupid raccoon. He'll chomp your eye out!

"Fuck him. He's my monkey and that's my beer. And this hairy, no-language-using, lower primate is about to get served up a big plate of homo-sapiens whoop ass!"

You broke eye contact! Never break eye contact! You fool! Look out!

[wild screeching]

Oh no! No! This is terrible. Oh God, no! The monkey is tearing at his face.

Oh, the humanity!

[vaguely human shrieks of bloodcurdling mayhem]

Just let him keep the beer. Let him keep it!

Everyone, run for your lives!

PUBLIC SERVICE ANNOUNCEMENT: If more people would just take the time to talk to their monkeys . . . Talk to your monkey.

But DO NOT give your monkey beer. Ever. No matter how cute he looks in a sailor suit. If you give that monkey beer, he will love it. He will begin to drink like us, become like us, and one day *speak* like us. Never give him beer. Do it for the Statue of Liberty.

LADIES' NIGHT

This book is intended

to be Man's guide to all things beer, but this section is dedicated to the ladies. Presented in the next few pages are ways for a woman to get the most out of beer, so that she too can love the precious fluid as much as we do.

Since the earliest days of brewing, women have had a vital role in delivering beer to Men. Though modern technology has made the female brewer all but extinct, your woman has not reached the state of total uselessness yet. There are some women out there who still possess the long-lost ability to *cook.*

Their numbers are dwindling, of course, but if you have in your possession a woman with cooking skills, count your blessings. The sad truth is most women today can't tell a colander from a Crock-Pot. There are many theories as to why the woman/cook is nearing extinction: They've joined the work force and don't have time; they never learned from their mothers; they're lazy. Certainly all of these theories have merit, but it's time we discussed the *real* reason.

If "cooking" to your woman consists of opening the box and setting the microwave to a minute-thirty, then *you* must accept some responsibility. As a Man, you've failed in your duties and allowed this situation to happen. Shame on *you,* for not directing your wife, girlfriend, or cellmate to her biological calling.

Luckily Woman, like any other species, can *learn.* Certainly not how a four-stroke engine works, or the importance of pitching in the post season, but she can learn *simple* things like the recipes presented here. There's plenty of beer in these recipes to help you get through it together, but you must be patient with her. For most women, being in the kitchen is like being in Albania.

When this section is put to proper use, you and your woman will develop a closer and more meaningful relationship.

BEER CAN CHICKEN

YOU'LL NEED:

1 chicken, 3 1/2 to 4 lbs.

1 can of beer (choose a brand he likes)

olive oil

3 cloves garlic, crushed

fresh basil

cayenne pepper

salt and pepper

HERE'S WHAT YOU DO:

Start with a hot grill. The grill is usually Man's domain, so don't screw it up: Make sure the coals are completely *white* before you begin cooking.

Remove about 1/4 - 1/2 of the beer from the can. Do NOT drink it, because you're starting to get fat. Perhaps you should put it in a glass with another 12 to 16 ounces and serve it to your Man.

Now prep the chicken. Rinse it, trim away some of the fat. Rub it liberally with your favorite meat rub. Rubbing the meat may not seem like your kind of thing, but trust me, he'll appreciate it.

Try this for your meat rub: olive oil, basil, fresh pressed garlic, salt, and plenty of cayenne pepper. If you really don't love him and are just doing this so he'll buy you something nice on Valentine's Day, you can purchase a ready-made seasoning mix at the store.

Using a can opener, open up a couple extra holes in the top of the can and drop the crushed garlic in with the beer. Speaking of which, your Man is probably ready for another one. Hop to it.

Lube up the can with olive oil. Now, make that chicken your bitch and work the upright can into its body cavity. If it gives you too much resistance, just pull the legs apart and shove it in. You know the drill. Once in the bird, the beer can allows it to stand upright on the grill.

Cover your grill and cook the chicken until its wings are loose. Cook times will vary, but the breast meat should reach 160-165 degrees.

Serve with his favorite side dishes. However, *you* shouldn't eat too much because garlic makes you smell. In fact, maybe you should just have a salad.

For you ladies with advanced cooking skills who like to mix it up, here are a couple things he'll be sure to love. Try presoaking some mesquite chips in beer and putting them on the coals . . . and try not to talk so much.

Serves 2-4 people, depending on whether or not you screwed it up.

BEER PUFFS

GO OUT AND BUY:

1 cup beer

¼ pound butter

1 cup sifted flour

½ teaspoon salt

4 eggs

4 cans crabmeat (approximately 7 ounces each)

HERE'S WHAT YOU DO:

First of all, stop whining. It's very unattractive. It's game day and your Man and his four friends need nourishment. Are they supposed to starve for three hours?

Bring beer and butter to boil. Smells good, don't it? When the butter is completely melted, stir in the flour and salt. Cook over low heat. Stir the mixture gently. Think about how none of this would be possible without your Man/provider.

When the mixture leaves the side of the pan, remove it from heat. Beat in one egg at a time until dough is shiny.

Using a teaspoon, place dough balls about an inch apart on a buttered cookie sheet. Place in oven preheated to 450 degrees F. After ten minutes, reduce the temperature to 350 degrees F and let them bake for another ten minutes or until browned and free of moisture. Hey, how 'bout that, you're cooking! Good girl!

When the puffs have cooled, split them open and stuff them with precooked crabmeat or shrimp or any other desired filling.

Quickly put on something nice and present them to the men. Smile a lot and remember: Do *not* stand in front of the TV.

Yield: 60 to 80 small puffs and an appreciative pat on the ass.

CLAM AND BEER APPETIZERS

FIND:

1 stick softened butter ($1/2$ cup)

$1/2$ cup fine breadcrumbs

$1/2$ cup beer

1 small onion, minced

4 garlic cloves, minced

2 tablespoons minced fresh parsley

$1 1/2$ teaspoons Italian seasoning

$1/2$ teaspoon dried oregano

salt and fresh ground pepper

4 small cans ($6 1/2$ ounces each) minced clams, drained

sliced French bread (40 pieces)

Parmesan cheese

HERE'S WHAT YOU DO:

Let's be honest, you don't have most of these ingredients in your kitchen. Your only experience with breadcrumbs is picking them off your sweater after you've had the croissant in the morning, the muffin at 10:30, and that roll that came with the big tin of pasta you had for lunch. So, first thing you need to do is lay off the carbs.

Anyway, all these ingredients can be purchased at the grocery store. Don't panic, that's the same place you buy your coffee and ice cream, but you'll have to go over a couple aisles.

Preheat oven to 375 degrees F while you lightly grease a cookie sheet (that means use butter on it). Combine everything but the last three ingredients on your list in a bowl and mix well, adding salt and pepper to taste. Now, add the clams and blend thoroughly. If mixture seems too dry, moisten with more beer.

Spread the clam mix onto slices of French bread, or spoon into clamshells. Bake them on the cookie sheet for 10 minutes. During that time, you should quietly begin cleaning up the mess you've made. A good place to start is all the breadcrumbs you spilled because you don't know how to read the side of a measuring cup.

Remove the tray from the oven and fire up your broiler. Sprinkle each piece lightly with Parmesan cheese and broil until tops are golden brown. Serve immediately.

Now get back in the kitchen to fetch him another beer. Keep the beer coming, because no poker game is complete without it.

Yield: 40 pieces and maybe he won't forget your birthday.

COCONUT BEER SHRIMP

THE STUFF YOU SHOULD HAVE HAD:

4 eggs

1 cup beer

2$\frac{1}{2}$ teaspoons cayenne pepper

$\frac{1}{2}$ teaspoon paprika

$\frac{1}{2}$ teaspoon salt

1 teaspoon garlic powder

1$\frac{1}{4}$ cup all-purpose flour

2 tablespoons baking powder

50 large raw shrimp (tails on, peeled, deveined)

1$\frac{1}{2}$-2 cups shredded coconut

cooking oil

SAUCE:

2 cups pineapple marmalade

$\frac{1}{4}$ cup Dijon mustard

3 tablespoons shredded horseradish

HERE'S WHAT YOU DO:

Mix all of your seasonings together in a small dish. Combine eggs, beer, flour, baking powder, and 1 teaspoon of your mixed seasonings in a medium-sized bowl. Grab your blender—what do you mean you don't have one? Now you know what you're getting next Christmas.

Without putting on makeup, go to your neighbor's house, explain that you're tired of tramping around and that you're trying to become a proper woman. Ask if you can use their blender.

Blend well. Congratulations, you've just made beer batter.

Now, season the shrimp with the remaining 3 teaspoons of your seasoning mix. Take a shrimp, dunk it in the beer batter, and roll it in the shredded coconut until it's covered. Using your deep saucepan or deep fryer, heat the oil to 350 degrees F.

The oil should be at least 1½ inches deep, or just about up to your middle knuckle. Okay, that was a test. If you still *have* your finger, continue. If not, you'd better learn to give incredible blow jobs.

Gently drop a few shrimp into the fryer and cook them until golden brown. Remove and drain them on paper towels. Repeat. Serve. Return the blender.

DIPPING SAUCE:

Blend together sauce ingredients. Place in bowl.

Yield: 6 servings and, for some, a prosthetic finger.

GUINNESS & LAMB STEW

THINGS THAT FRIGHTEN YOU:

2 pounds lean stewing lamb

3 tablespoons oil

2 tablespoons flour

Salt and freshly ground pepper

2 large onions, coarsely chopped

2 cups small potatoes, peeled, quartered

1½ cups Guinness stout

2 cups carrots, chopped into chunks

Sprig of thyme

HERE'S WHAT YOU DO:

Trim the lamb of any fat or gristle. Cut the meat into cubes of about 1 1/2 inches and place them in a bowl with 1 tablespoon of oil. Add salt and freshly ground pepper to the flour, and toss the lamb into the mixture.

Using high heat and a wide frying pan, heat the remaining oil. Brown the meat on all sides, then add the onions, cover and cook gently for about five minutes.

Dump the contents of the pan into a casserole dish. Pour some of the Guinness into the frying pan. Bring the beer to a boil, stirring to dissolve the caramelized meat juices that are in the pan.

Pour contents from the pan onto the meat in the casserole dish. Add the remaining Guinness, carrots, potatoes, and thyme. Stir and add salt to taste.

The stew can now be cooked on top of the stove, or in a low oven at 300 degrees F. Cover with the casserole lid; simmer very gently until the meat is tender. You've got about two to three hours to kill.

So what are you going to do? I'll tell you what you're *not* gonna do. You're not going to sit on your ass in front of the television. How's this for a suggestion? Get on that cross-training thing that cost him a fortune but you just had to have, and take a nice jog around the living room. And while you're up there, see the sights: the dust on the floor, the dishes on the table, and the cat hair on the couch.

By the time you're finished doing the woman's work, it's time to taste your lamb stew and correct the seasoning. Scatter with lots of chopped parsley.

Yield: 6 to 8 servings and sore, but slightly tighter glutes.

WHAT BEER TO SERVE WITH FOOD

Good news, ladies, most of that troublesome *thinking* and *deciding* have already been done for you in this department. One of the many great things about foreigners is that they've already had *Men* figure out what kind of beer goes best with their food. Examples have been provided for you and placed in this handy list. It's so simple, even a woman such as you couldn't screw it up. So defrost some . . . and drink some.

Mexican:
Tacos, Burritos, Fajitas
Something light on the tongue that lets the spices come out, like a pale Mexican lager.
Try Tecate, Sol, or Pacifico.

Thai:
Hot & Sour Soup, Spicy Fish, Curries, Pad Thai
Crisp and *very* cold. The food is very hot and spicy and a cold beer cools the mouth. Besides, shitty *Thai* beer tastes better when cold.
Try Singha.

German:
Sauerbraten, Bratwurst & Sauerkraut, Potato Pancakes
A robust, hearty bock beer to go with the full-bodied flavor of the food.
Try Spaten.

American:

Fried Chicken, Hamburgers, Pizza, Sandwiches

An American brew with a full, flavorful, hoppy aroma that isn't too heavy.

Try Sierra Nevada or Brooklyn Lager in bottles.

Irish:

Boiled Potatoes, Twice Boiled Potatoes, Mashed Potatoes,
Twice Boiled Mashed Potatoes, Boiled Potato Mash with Cabbage

If you're serving Irish food, *don't*. It's because of Irish cooking that Guinness has come to replace meals. If you insist on boiling meat and vegetables until they're reduced to a flavorless slush and calling it "dinner," he's gonna want *whiskey* to go with it—John Power & Son Whiskey, triple distilled, matured in oak casks since 1791.

TEN RESPONSES FOR WHEN HE YELLS "GIMME A BEER!"

Sometimes when he barks at you to get him a beer, you freeze up and stare at him with a strange look on your face. This is a common reaction when women like you are surprised or confused. Though getting a beer *seems* like a pretty uncomplicated task, for some women even this makes them recoil into uncertainty about what to say or do next. It's okay. *It's a woman's right to be indecisive.* Thankfully, now you can learn this list of easily memorized responses to his simple request.

1. Are you sure one will be enough? You do have *two* hands.

2. Mmm . . . It really turns me on when you boss me around.

3. Okay, but when I'm done, can I please do some more laundry?

4. Great! But remember, tonight's my night to sit quietly and watch *Sports Center.*

5. If you insist, but I was really hoping to give you oral sex for a couple hours.

6. You're so smart! I knew I had some kind of purpose around here! (This response should be accompanied by a cute jiggle of your boobs.)

7. Right away! Oh, and by the way I've decided I don't need any more jewelry or new clothes.

8. Yes, dear. But would you mind if I *didn't* tell you about my day?

9. Okay, but hurry up and drink it, because my (friend, sister, or the babysitter) is coming over for our three-way.

10. Of course. But none for me, I've got another hour to do on the treadmill.

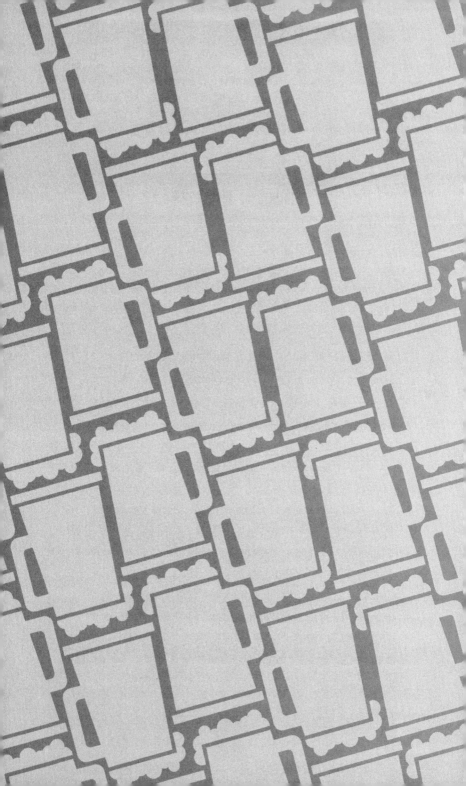

GLOSSARY

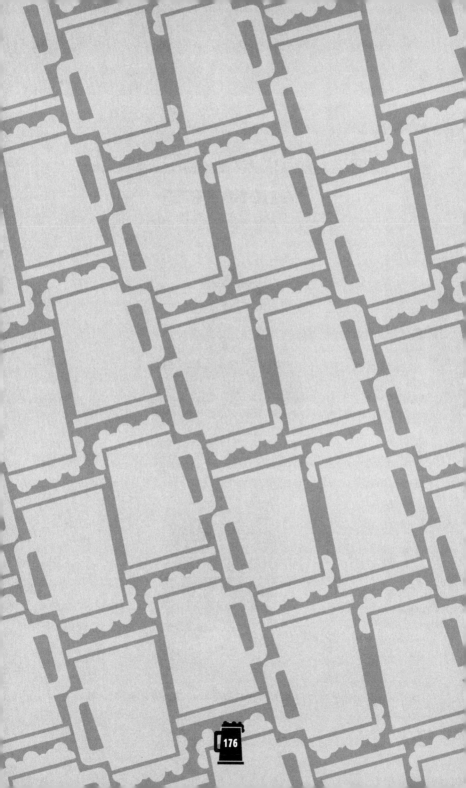

Ale: The English language term for a brew made with a top-fermenting yeast. Ales are produced in a wide variety of colors, palates, and strengths. An ale is a great place to start if you want to get shit-faced alphabetically.

Beer coat: The warm but invisible coat worn on a cold night that is created by the heat you give off after many hours of drinking. Usually, relying on a beer coat is a great way to get hypothermia.

Beer compass: An internal, invisible navigational device that ensures our safe arrival at home after a night of heavy drinking, even though we're too loaded to remember where we live, how we get there, and where we've come from.

Beer shits: The name guys who quite regularly have leaky stools and skid-marked boxers have given the form of excrement they create after a night of heavy drinking. Can also be accomplished by spending several weeks writing a book while drinking nothing but beer.

Bitter: A very hoppy ale that's usually served on tap. The extra hops are what give this medium-strength, dark-colored brew its characteristic bitterness. Bitters come from England, a cold, unwelcoming country full of drunken fanatics who can obsess about anything. It doesn't matter if it's Buddy Holly or bar towels. In England you'll find more aficionado pub-rats per capita, by far, than anywhere else in the world . . . except perhaps for Ireland, Germany, or Australia.

Bock: Usually a dark, bottom-fermented brew from barley malt. Its name comes from the German term for "strong beer." Beer to the Germans is like snow to the Eskimo—they've got nearly 250 words for it. The only difference is the Eskimo gets drunk with two beers, and the German gets drunk with power.

Boot: To puke.

Brown ale: A dark brown ale, sweet in palate, and of only moderate alcohol content ranging from 3-4.5%. Very popular in England. You'd probably need ten to twelve of these before you'd be really ready to bash some fan of Manchester United in the face with your steel-toed boots.

Butcher: A name for a small glass of beer in South Australia. The term allegedly comes from the theory that a butcher could take a quick break from his job, have a drink, and be right back to work. In the States, we'd call this same type of beer a "Chicago Cop."

Cask-conditioned (ale): Draught beer that has been neither filtered nor pasteurized, and has a secondary fermentation and precipitation of yeast in a vented cask. It's the fabled stuff that you'd find in the cellar of a classic pub. So you'll probably never experience it. It probably tastes great, but this "secondary fermentation" stuff is the kind of thing that guys with big bellies, beards, and thick sweaters talk about when they get online in a beer-nerd chat room.

Church key: Term for that thing your grandmother was always looking for when she was trying to tie one on. This device was the tool of choice that answered the thirsty drinker's prayers before the invention of the twist-off cap.

Dry beer: Originally, "dry beer" was a milder Japanese version of an already mild German beer. With the great success of dry beer's marketing in Japan, the term was jumped upon by American megabrewers who used it to peddle another version that's even *more* mild. Beer aficionados complain that this beer has "no finish," which, to the rest of us, means it's got all the flavor of a regular beer that's been pissed back into the bottle.

Eisbock: A double (*doppel*) strong German bock beer with an increased alcohol content due to a freezing process. Because water freezes before alcohol, it can be converted to ice (*eis*) and removed from the mixture, leaving behind a greater concentration of alcohol. It's all about purity with the Germans, so the ice is rounded up and usually never seen again.

Genuine draft: Term for a bottled or canned beer that, like most draughts, isn't pasteurized. The rub is that they *sterile filter* all the live yeasts and beer-makin' cooties out of the mix instead, to give it a longer shelf life. In other words, this is another corporate-pimped term that holds out the promise of an authentically different beer experience, without actually delivering. Tricked again!

Gusto: This is what you were allegedly "going for" when you grabbed a Schlitz. When the company was notified that, in another language, this word means "taste," they immediately dropped the ad campaign for fear of false advertising litigation.

Heffeweizen: An increasingly popular wheat (*weizen*) beer that has been sedimented with yeast. Known to have a tart, fruity, sometimes spicy palate. The story is, German beer scientists developed this style long ago by doing countless tests on identical twins . . . and then having a beer.

Herniated disc: The injury that befalls the guy who chose the wrong two people to hold his legs during an ill-fated kegstand. Can occur in a woman, too, but she'd have to be really overweight.

India Pale Ale: The IPA is familiar to most as the American version of the British pale ales, which were given extra hops to protect the beer on its trip to India. Once in India, the warm, supercharged brew with a 5% alcohol content was guzzled down by soldiers and diplomats who'd gladly give a week's pay to shit in something other than a sacred river.

Kellerbier: Another German term, this one indicating an unfiltered lager, usually with a high hop content and low carbonation.

Klosterbier: German term meaning "cloister beer," for a beer that is, or once was, produced in a monastery or convent, by people whose devotion to beer is second only to their devotion to God . . . or anyone with shiny black boots.

Krausenbier: Yet another German beer that uses some crazy ancient brewing process in the making of yet another fantastic brew. This time we end up with an unfiltered beer that was given carbonation by adding unfermented malt sugars to the conditioning tank. But you can't help but feel that it's called *krausenbier* because Germans can't get through a day without inventing another scary sounding "k" word by mid-afternoon.

Lager: This is about as "meat and potatoes" as you can get for a beer, encompassing any beer that is brewed by bottom fermentation. Can be either light or dark in color. In Germany this is beer for foreigners.

Lambic: A type of spontaneously fermenting wheat beer from Belgium. Like many Belgians, this beer takes great offense at being mistaken for French. Similar to how a Moosehead would feel if you were to mistake it for a Bud.

Light beer: Before the Atkins diet declared war on America's last pleasure land, carbs, this was the beer of choice for calorie-counting guys who should seriously consider just going ahead with the sex change. They've basically traded in about 45 calories per can to drink something that *real* beer lovers would call "backwash." Seriously, gentle reader, this may be the last chance in the book to say this, *you guys are not Men.*

Malt liquor: Despite its name, this brew is not malty, and can contain large amounts of cheaper sugars. You know what else? It's technically not a *liquor,* either. Nope, it's just a kickass version of a regular American lager. Intended for a cheap "high," it's marketed toward African Americans because, for a black guy, malt liquor will cause what's probably the least of his life's many headaches.

Manpole: 1. The metal bar Foosball men are attached to. 2. The thing Foosball fanatics secretly crave.

Pilsner: Inspired by a famous brew from the Czech town of Pilsen, in the province of Bohemia, these are bottom-fermenting beers characterized by their hoppiness and golden color. Pilsners are known for their distinctive aroma, just like the Czechs.

Porter: Similar to a lighter-bodied stout, this London-born beer has gone pretty much extinct save for those brewed by American microbrewers like Sierra Nevada. There may be hope for us yet.

Schooner: A large beer glass in Queensland; a medium beer glass in South Australia. They're very macho down there in South Australia, where catching a crocodile is only step 1 toward fucking it.

Skull: More Aussie slang, this time for drinking a beer in a single pull, without taking a breath, as in, to "skull a beer." "Skull—it's Australian for chug."

Steam beer: Anchor Steam Beer of San Francisco copyrighted this name for their method of bottom fermentation at high temperatures in unusually wide, shallow vessels. It's claimed that early California brewers, who lacked access to ice, used this method as they tried to make the elusive bottom-fermenting beer. The beer was said to "steam" when the casks were tapped and to this day, for a select subset of men, San Francisco is the mecca for steamy bottom fermenting.

Stout: An extra-dark, top-fermenting brew, made with highly roasted malts. Surprisingly, the American version of this fave can contain more of that sweet, sweet alcohol than comparable stouts found in England. The good ol' US of A packs more than 5% alcohol in their stouts, while the English weigh in at about 3.75%. For a Brit, every day means facing the haunting, inescapable reality that they haven't been a world power since the Great War. However, things are different in some tropical countries, where Guinness stout can have an alcohol content over 8% . . . and twice the number of kids.

Stubby: Charming Australian slang for a 375-milliliter beer bottle. Now, go find a *different* book that can explain just how much 375 milliliters is.

Tasteless: 1. Term used to characterize a beer without distinctive flavor. See "Pilsner, American." 2. In poor taste, lacking refinement. *Example:* Q. "What's the difference between a beer and a gay guy?" A. "One comes in a can, and sometimes the other can't come in the can."

Trappist: The famous order of monks whose breweries in Belgium and the Netherlands maintain legal exclusivity over the Trappist name applied to their flavorful, top-fermenting, bottle-conditioned beer. Yes, it's particularly strong (up to 12% alcohol by volume), but what does this complex, distinctive monk mix mean to you and me? For starters, you can get the same brain-stabbing hangover you get from malt liquor at nearly three times the price.

Weisse: A pale beer made from wheat named after the German term *weisse,* for "white." Uncharacteristic for Germany, a beer's religion, unlike its color, has little factor in how it's classified.

Witbier: A Dutch/Flemish term for describing a "wheat beer" used in Belgium and increasingly by Americans, most of whom probably couldn't find Dutchland or Flemia on a map.

Z

Zwickelbier: Every glossary needs at least one entry under "Z," so here it is. This is a German term for an unfiltered beer without the distinguishing features of either a keller-bier or a krausenbier. Sometimes I think the Germans are just making this stuff up.

From the writer ...

Thanks to:
Tom Gianas, Robert Smigel, Everyone from
The Man Show 2.0, Scott Stone, David Stanely,
Matthew Marcus, Dawn Lach
Ryan Harbage
John Powers & Sons
Doug Stanhope and Joe Rogan
Jimmy, Adam, and Daniel for creating something
I've had the good fortune to be a part of.
My family
Special thanks to Tracy for her patience and support.

Additional thanks to:
Everyone at Stone Stanley Entertainment, David Decker,
Jennifer Decker, Eliot Goldberg, Sharon Levy, Kira
Wagner, Jason Burch, Dan Helberg, Stephanie Gutierrez,
Tricia Boczkowski. Everyone at Comedy Central, Jason
Korfine, Rob LaQuinta, and Margaret Milnes

Ray James is a

consulting producer for *The Man Show* and has been a staff writer on *The Daily Show, Saturday Night Live,* and *TV Funhouse* as well as countless other TV shows you've probably never heard of, seen, or liked. In addition to writing for television, he coproduced the "Come Poop With Me" CD by Triumph the Insult Comic Dog, for which he cowrote many of the songs. If you see him in your travels, don't hesitate to buy him a beer.